# MAYBE THIS IS LOVE

## DARSHA S NAIR

TO MOM AND DAD

THIS FIRST ONE IS

FOR YOU

Copyright © 2025> <Darsha S Nair>



Made with ❤ on the Notion Press Platform

www.notionpress.com

# Contents

CONTENTS



Epilogue

# Foreword

Stories have an incredible way of reflecting our own emotions, even when we least expect them to. They remind us of who we once were, who we are now, and the countless moments that shape us along the way. Some stories make us smile, others make us ache, and a rare few leave us with an undeniable feeling that we've lived through them ourselves. *Maybe This Is Love* is one of those rare stories.

At its heart, this book is about love—not just the love we find in romance, but the love we share in friendships, in fleeting moments, in the silent understanding between two people, and even in the memories that refuse to fade. It is a story about growing up, about discovering who we are, and about learning that life doesn't always go the way we imagined it would. It explores the joy of feeling deeply, the pain of letting go, and the uncertainty of what comes next.

There comes a time in everyone's life when the world begins to shift. The friendships we once thought were permanent begin to change. The people we never imagined losing start to drift away. The dreams we once chased so fearlessly start to evolve into something different. It's in these moments that we begin to understand that life is not always about holding on—sometimes, it's about learning to let go. *Maybe This Is*

*Love* beautifully captures this transition, painting a picture of love, loss, and the lingering emotions that stay with us long after we say goodbye.

Darsha S Nair writes with a depth of emotion that makes her characters feel real, as if they could be people we know—or even reflections of ourselves. Her storytelling is gentle yet powerful, drawing readers into a world that feels familiar, a world where love is both breathtaking and heartbreaking, where friendships feel like home, and where life's unexpected turns leave us wondering what could have been. Her words remind us of the unspoken feelings we've all experienced—the hesitation before saying how we truly feel, the quiet heartbreak of drifting apart, and the small moments that change everything, even when we don't realize it at the time.

What makes this book so special is not just the story it tells, but the emotions it evokes. It is not just a love story; it is a story about growing up, about discovering ourselves, about the people who shape us, and the ones who leave footprints on our hearts. It is about the moments we cherish, the ones we regret, and the ones we never forget. It asks a question that lingers long after the final page: *Was it love, or was it just a moment in time?*

To every reader who picks up this book, I hope you find a piece of yourself in these pages. Whether it reminds you of your own friendships, your own heartbreaks, or the love that almost was, let this story take you on a journey— one that will stay with you long after the last word is read.

Darsha S Nair

23.3.25

# Preface

Stories often begin in the quietest moments—through fleeting glances, whispered conversations, and the emotions we carry but rarely say aloud. *Maybe This Is Love* was born from these very moments, from the realization that love and friendship are not always about grand gestures but about the small, everyday moments that shape us in ways we don't fully understand until much later.

When I first started writing this book, I didn't have a perfect story in mind. I only had a feeling—one that lingered, one that made me think about the friendships we assume will last forever, the love we are sometimes too afraid to acknowledge, and the way life has a habit of changing everything before we're ready. I wanted to capture that fleeting, bittersweet reality—of growing up, of moving forward, of realizing that even the strongest connections can fade, not because they were never real, but because life has a way of pulling people in different directions.

The characters in this book are not based on any one person, but they hold emotions, thoughts, and struggles that are deeply human. At their core, they represent the feelings we have all experienced at some point—the hesitation before saying what we truly feel, the uncertainty of not knowing where we stand with someone, and the quiet heartbreak of watching people drift away. Through their journeys, I hope to explore the beauty and pain of love in all its forms—the kind found in friendships, in fleeting moments, in the unspoken words between two people, and in the memories that stay with us long after someone is gone.

Writing this book has been a journey of reflection, of reliving emotions that I, too, have felt at different points in my life. It wasn't just about creating a story; it was about putting into words the thoughts and emotions that often remain unspoken. In doing so, I realized how universal these experiences are—how we have all, at some point, loved and lost, hoped and hesitated, held on and let go. And perhaps, that is what makes love so special—not its permanence, but its impact.

To those who pick up this book, I hope it resonates with you in some way. I hope it reminds you of the friendships that shaped you, the love that changed you, and the moments that made you who you are. Whether you read it as a reflection of your past, a reminder of your present, or a glimpse into what the future might hold, my greatest wish is that this story stays with you long after the final page is turned.

Thank you for being a part of this journey.

*Darsha S Nair*

23.5.2025

# Acknowledgments

Writing a book is never a solitary journey, and *Maybe This Is Love* would not have been possible without the love, support, and encouragement of so many people. As I reflect on this journey, I am filled with gratitude for those who have been by my side every step of the way.

First and foremost, my heartfelt thanks go to my parents. Your unwavering belief in me has been the foundation of everything I do. Thank you for always encouraging me to dream, to create, and to follow my passion for writing. Your love, patience, and endless support have given me the strength to keep going, even when self-doubt crept in. This book is as much yours as it is mine.

To my friends, thank you for being my greatest sources of inspiration. Through your laughter, your kindness, and even your challenges, you have helped shape the emotions and relationships in this story. Whether you knew it or not, your words, your experiences, and the memories we've shared found their way into these pages in some form. Thank you for always supporting me, for listening to my endless ideas, and for reminding me why I love storytelling in the first place.

ACKNOWLEDGMENTS

To my family, thank you for your constant encouragement and for always believing in my writing. Your faith in me has meant more than I can ever express. Every word I write carries a piece of the love and support you have given me throughout my life.

And finally, to you—the readers. You are the reason this book exists beyond my own imagination. Thank you for picking up this story, for allowing these characters to become a part of your world, and for feeling every joy, heartbreak, and moment of growth along with them. Writing is nothing without readers, and I am endlessly grateful to each and every one of you for giving this book a place in your hearts.

This journey has been filled with moments of doubt, excitement, and discovery, and I would not have made it here without all of you. From the bottom of my heart, thank you for being a part of it.

# Prologue/Introduction

The cameras flashed, the crowd murmured, and the interviewer leaned forward with a knowing smile.

"Alright, Caleb," she said, adjusting her cue cards. "Your band Eclipse Crew has taken the world by storm. Millions of fans, sold-out stadiums, and a chart-topping album. But let's talk about something more personal."

Caleb Miller, now twenty, leaned back in his chair, a faint smirk playing on his lips. Dressed in a sleek black suit, with his signature messy hair and easy charm, he looked every bit the global sensation he had become. But there was something in his eyes—something distant.

The interviewer glanced at her notes before asking the question that sent the room into silence.

"Who was your first love?"

For a moment, Caleb didn't speak. He could hear the buzz of the cameras, the quiet anticipation from the crew, the faint hum of a song playing somewhere in the background. But in his mind, he was no longer here.

# 1. 2 Souls

"I swear, if Mr. Carter gives us one more essay, I'm running away," Sophie groaned, shutting her locker with a dramatic sigh.

Lily Parker laughed, adjusting the strap of her backpack. "You've been saying that since freshman year. Still here, though."

Sophie rolled her eyes. "That's because I have no choice. But seriously, do teachers think we don't have lives?"

Lily smiled but didn't reply. Instead, she glanced around the crowded hallway of Maplewood High. Students shuffled to their classes, some chatting, some half-asleep, some scrambling to finish homework at the last minute. Just another ordinary morning.

A few feet away, Caleb walked through the entrance, slipping his headphones off as he headed toward his locker. Mornings weren't his thing, and neither was unnecessary conversation. He preferred the quiet—books, music, and football. Unlike Sophie and Lily, who filled the halls with laughter, Caleb kept to himself.

They didn't know each other. They had no reason to. Just two students moving through their own lives.

"Sup Caleb" said James, Caleb's good old buddy or maybe the only buddy he has.

"Oh, hey man" replied Caleb. "How was Tokyo? Saw those clicks on your id."

"Oh, hell yeah dude. Tokyo was legit. The food and the culture man like it's just so fascinating and learnt some Japanese! Konnichiwa Caleb-San, Ariga-

"Good morning, everyone. Here are today's updates." the speaker interrupting James. "First, a reminder that the science club meeting will take place in MT 12 during lunch break. Members, please be on time. Next, the inter-house debate competition, which was originally scheduled for today, has been postponed to Friday. The new timings will be put up on the notice board, so be sure to check."

Just as he was about to move on, the microphone crackled, and a voice interrupted him mid-sentence.

"Excuse me kid, sorry to interrupt," Mr. Carter's voice came through the speaker. "I have an important announcement to add."

"It's Miguel" the announcer murmured, side eyeing Mr. Carter

The announcer stepped back, letting him continue.

"Students, listen up! The Annual Sports Day competition is officially scheduled for the 6th of March!"

A murmur of excitement spread through the crowd.

"Those interested in participating must sign up at the sports office by the end of the day. Practice sessions will begin this week, so get ready!"

"Damn, well you are applying ain't ya?" said James

"Nah, not interested James San" he replied mockingly

"Oh hell nah boy, you ARE applying and you better listen man! You do realize that being a nerd = a dork with no girl. It's high time that you ENLIGHTEN yourself with some swag plus we all know that you real good in football!" responded James now being in action of mocking Caleb

"Alright, alright. I'll do it. Not because I care or anything—just so you stop bugging me."

(grinning) "Yeah, sure, totally not because you care." Replied James

"Whatever, man. Just tell me where to sign up." rolling his eyes replied Caleb

"Oo sports day competition! You are applying right Sophie? You gotta show those basketball skills!" asked lily

"WELL as much as I would love to participate, I'm leaving for California on 5th of march." Replied Sophie

"Woah! What for?"

"I got selected for that international basketball tournament remember?"

"Oh yeah! well congratulations once again…" sighed lily

"Alright, what's up?" she asked, nudging Lily's arm.

Lily hesitated, staring at the ground. "It's nothing."

Sophie raised an eyebrow. "Lily."

Lily sighed again, this time heavier. "It's just… everyone's so excited about Sports Day, signing up for events, forming teams… and I'm just gonna be there, standing around, alone."

Sophie tilted her head. "Alone? What are you talking about?"

Lily shrugged. "You're not gonna be here. And me? I have nothing. I'm just going to watch while mostly everyone else actually does something."

Sophie was quiet for a moment, then bumped her shoulder lightly against Lily's. "First of all, you're never alone." She grinned. "Second, you don't have to compete to enjoy Sports Day. It's not just about running or jumping—it's about being there, cheering, laughing, having fun. And trust me, they all are going to need you a nerd yelling at them to run faster."

Lily huffed a small laugh. "I maybe do give the best motivational speeches."

"Exactly!" Sophie said, smiling. "Think of it as a very important job."

Lily rolled her eyes but smiled. "Fine. I guess I won't be completely useless."

Sophie looped an arm around Lily's shoulders. "See? It's settled. "

Lily smiled and playfully hit Sophie's arm. "You're so dramatic."

Sophie gasped, pretending to be offended. "Excuse you, I was giving an inspirational speech!"

Lily laughed, shaking her head. Maybe Sports Day wouldn't be so bad after all.

# 2. Seen, Yet Unseen

The sports field buzzed with energy as students and teachers gathered for the biggest event of the year—Sports Day. Banners fluttered in the breeze, and the rhythmic beat of the school drum echoed across the ground, signalling the start of the competitions. The air smelled of freshly cut grass and excitement.

Caleb stood by the sidelines, adjusting his jersey as the football match was about to begin. His team huddled together; eyes sharp with determination. He exhaled, rolling his shoulders, but something felt off. He turned his head slightly, scanning the crowd.

James wasn't beside him.

Instead, he spotted his friend up in the school gallery, sitting stiffly in the stands. Caleb's gaze lingered for a second, remembering why James wasn't on the field. A major injury during practice had ruled him out of the competition. Caleb had seen how much it had frustrated James, how much he had wanted to be out there, playing alongside him.

Now, instead of standing on the sidelines, rallying the team, he was forced to watch from a distance, his leg wrapped in a brace. But when he caught Caleb's searching gaze, he still managed a grin, raising a fist in encouragement.

Caleb frowned for a moment, then smirked. Typical James. Even injured, he refused to sit quietly.

Shaking his head, Caleb refocused as the referee blew the whistle, signalling the start of the game. The crowd erupted as the match began, the ball darting from one player to another in a blur of speed and strategy.

Meanwhile, on the track, the 100-meter sprinters took their positions. The announcer's voice boomed over the microphone. "On your marks… get set… GO!" The runners exploded forward, their legs pumping, the crowd cheering them on.

Across the field, the long jump event was underway, competitors sprinting down the runway before leaping into the sand pit. The measuring tape was pulled tight, judges calling out distances.

Back at the football match, Caleb dribbled past a defender, his pulse pounding in his ears. He saw an opening and took the shot. The ball soared through the air—straight into the net.

"YES!" The crowd roared, and Caleb instinctively looked toward the gallery. James was on his feet now—well, as much as he could be—arms raised in triumph, yelling something inaudible but unmistakably celebratory.

Caleb grinned, relief and exhilaration washing over him. Maybe James wasn't on the field, but he was still right there, cheering him on in his own way.

Sports Day had only just begun, and the competition was fiercer than ever.

The football match was in full swing, the intensity on the field growing with every passing minute. Caleb wiped sweat from his brow as he scanned the crowd for James. He had been right beside him just a moment ago, but now he was nowhere to be seen.

His eyes trailed up to the school gallery, searching for his friend. Instead, his gaze landed on someone else.

Lily Parker.

Even from a distance, she stood out. The sunlight filtered through the open-air gallery, casting a golden glow on her auburn hair, making it shimmer like autumn leaves caught in the breeze. The wind played with the loose strands, framing her delicate features—soft eyes that held an unreadable expression, lips slightly parted as if lost in thought. She sat alone, her posture slouched, eyes fixed on the field but not really watching.

Caleb knew that look—disinterest masked as focus. The usual spark she carried during Sports Day was missing. He remembered hearing something about her best friend, Sophie, leaving for a basketball tournament in California. Maybe that was why she looked a little… lost.

Another whistle from the referee snapped him back to the game.

"Caleb! Focus!" someone shouted.

He shook his head, pushing the thought aside. There was a match to win. But as he turned back to the field, he couldn't quite shake the image of Lily sitting there, lost in a crowd full of noise.

Moments later, the opportunity came. Caleb dodged past a defender, his pulse pounding in his ears. He saw an opening and took the shot. The ball soared through the air—straight into the net.

The crowd erupted. Cheers rang out across the field, but one voice stood out to him.

Lily.

She had jumped to her feet, her earlier stillness gone. Her hands cupped around her mouth as she cheered along with the rest of the students, her eyes finally alive with excitement. For the first time that day, she didn't look lonely—she looked radiant.

Caleb grinned, the rush of the goal mixing with something else—a warmth he hadn't expected. Maybe, just maybe, Sports Day wasn't going to be so ordinary after all.

The final whistle blew, and the stadium erupted in cheers. Caleb's team had won. His teammates rushed toward him, shouting and clapping him on the back, but his mind was elsewhere.

As the celebrations unfolded, his gaze instinctively drifted back to the gallery.

Lily Parker.

She was standing now, her face lit up with a brilliant smile, hands clapping with genuine excitement. The way her eyes sparkled, the way her laughter blended with the roar of the crowd—it was mesmerizing. Caleb had never really paid much attention to her before, but at this moment, he couldn't look away.

And then, she looked at him.

For just a second, their eyes locked. The noise of the field faded into the background, and all he could see was her—radiant, beautiful, glowing in the afternoon sunlight. His heart stuttered in his chest, an unfamiliar warmth spreading through him.

Was this… love at first sight?

The thought startled him. He barely knew Lily, yet here he was, completely captivated by her smile.

Before he could process it further, a weight dropped around his neck—the championship medal. Someone had handed it to him, but his mind was still caught in that fleeting moment.

Then—whack!

"Earth to Caleb," James chuckled, smacking his hand playfully. "You good, champ? You look like you just saw a ghost."

Caleb blinked, shaking himself back to reality. "Uh—yeah. Just… taking it all in."

James smirked. "Sure, sure. Or were you taking in something else?"

Caleb rolled his eyes, adjusting his medal, but his gaze flickered back to the gallery one last time.

Lily was still smiling.

And for some reason, he couldn't stop smiling either.

As Caleb approached his block, an unsettling feeling settled deep within him. No matter how hard he tried, his thoughts kept circling back to Lily. It was frustrating—this wasn't him. He was the kind of guy who had everything under control, the one who always had his priorities straight. But right now, his mind felt like a tangled mess.

Shaking his head, he exhaled sharply and forced himself to focus. His exams were just around the corner, and as a topper, he couldn't afford to let distractions creep in. He wasn't about to let fleeting emotions derail everything he had worked so hard for. Yet, despite his best efforts, a part of him couldn't shake the strange, unfamiliar pull she had on him.

James watched Caleb closely as they walked through the corridor. It wasn't like him to be this absentminded— usually, he was the one reminding everyone else to stay focused. But today, Caleb seemed distant, lost in thought, barely acknowledging the world around him.

Frowning, James nudged his shoulder. "Hey, you good?"

Caleb blinked, snapping out of his daze. "Huh? Yeah… yeah, I'm fine," he muttered, though his voice lacked its usual confidence.

James wasn't convinced. "Come on, man. You've been weirdly quiet. What's up?"

Caleb hesitated for a moment, then sighed. "It's nothing. Just… trying to focus on exams now."

James raised an eyebrow. "You? Distracted about exams right after sports day? Now I know something's up." He crossed his arms. "Is it a person?"

Caleb stiffened slightly, but the flicker in his eyes gave him away.

James smirked. "It is a person, isn't it?"

Caleb groaned, rubbing his temple. "It's nothing, James. Drop it."

James chuckled. "Oh, this is gonna be fun."

# 3. Reactions and Realizations

The air in the science block buzzed with quiet anticipation as students shuffled into the laboratory, their crisp white coats a stark contrast against the dark countertops. Beakers clinked, burners flickered, and the faint scent of chemicals lingered in the air—a familiar yet intimidating prelude to the practical assessment.

Today marked the beginning of the 11th graders' examinations, starting with the much-dreaded science practical. For weeks, students had poured over their notes, memorizing formulas, reaction mechanisms, and lab procedures, but now, it was time to put theory into action. Precision, accuracy, and composure were key—one wrong measurement, and an entire experiment could go awry.

Caleb took a deep breath as he stepped into the lab, shaking off the distractions that had plagued him for days. This was his domain. Here, logic reigned, and emotions had no place. He rolled his shoulders, adjusting his grip on his lab journal, and for the first time in what felt like ages, he felt like himself again. The strange turmoil he had been battling was still there, lurking beneath the surface, but for now, he chose to set it aside.

Right now, there was only science—measurable, predictable, and entirely within his control. Or so he thought.

As Caleb set up his workstation, carefully arranging the beakers and measuring cylinders, James slid into the seat beside him, smirking.

"So… you gonna tell me who's been messing with your head, or do I have to guess?" James teased, adjusting his lab coat.

Caleb sighed, rolling his eyes. "James, we have a practical assessment to focus on. Maybe try worrying about your titration instead of my life?"

James chuckled. "Oh, come on. You, of all people, getting distracted before an exam? That's big news. It's gotta be someone special." He leaned in, lowering his voice. "Is it a she?"

Caleb stiffened for a fraction of a second before resuming his work, meticulously pouring a solution into a flask. "I don't know what you're talking about," he muttered.

James grinned. "Oh, you so do."

Caleb shot him a warning look. "James, if you mess up your readings because you're too busy being annoying, I'm not helping you fix them."

James put his hands up in mock surrender. "Fine, fine. I'll back off… for now." He picked up his burette, a playful glint still in his eyes. "But you will talk. It's only a matter of time."

Caleb shook his head, exhaling slowly. He needed to focus. Science was his safe space—logical, structured, predictable.

Unlike whatever was happening in his head whenever he thought about her.

As Caleb carefully adjusted the pipette, trying to drown out James' smirks and his own wandering thoughts, a familiar voice interrupted his concentration.

"Mr. Miller," Mr. Carter's deep, authoritative tone cut through the low murmurs in the lab. Caleb straightened instinctively, turning to face his science teacher. Mr. Carter stood with his arms crossed, surveying him with a keen, knowing gaze.

"Are you prepared for today's assessment?" the teacher asked, his voice carrying both expectation and challenge.

Caleb gave a small nod. "Yes, sir. I've revised all the experiments thoroughly."

Mr. Carter hummed in approval, glancing over Caleb's neatly arranged workstation. "Good. I wouldn't expect anything less from you." Then, after a brief pause, he added, "Though you seem a little… distracted today."

Caleb stiffened slightly but quickly composed himself. "Just going over the procedure in my head, sir."

Mr. Carter raised an eyebrow, unconvinced. "I see. Well, let me remind you—science is about precision, not preoccupation. Whatever is on your mind, leave it outside the lab." His tone wasn't harsh, but there was a weight to it, a subtle warning.

Caleb nodded. "Yes, sir."

Mr. Carter studied him for another second before his expression softened. "I know you aim for perfection, Caleb, but don't forget—science isn't just about getting everything right. It's about understanding, adapting. If you spend too much time in your head, you'll miss what's right in front of you."

Something about those words hit differently. Caleb wasn't sure if Mr. Carter was talking about the experiment or something else entirely. Either way, he pushed aside the thoughts of Lily that had been clouding his mind and focused on what was in front of him—his experiment, his work, his control.

"Understood, sir," he said firmly, gripping his pipette with renewed determination.

Mr. Carter gave a small nod before walking away, leaving Caleb with a little more clarity than before.

As the last drop of solution settled in the beaker, Caleb noted his final observation, double-checking his calculations with a small, satisfied smile. The practical was over, and he had managed to stay completely focused. No distractions, no misplaced thoughts—just science. See? It was just a small crush. Nothing worth losing my mind over.

As soon as he stepped out of the lab, though, he spotted James leaning casually against the wall, arms crossed, wearing the biggest smirk possible.

"There he is! The future Nobel Prize winner. So… did all those chemical reactions help you neutralize your feelings?" James wiggled his eyebrows dramatically.

Caleb groaned. "I'm leaving."

He turned on his heel, but James was faster, falling into step beside him. "Aw, come on, don't run away! I just want to know if she was still in your head while you were mixing all those solutions."

"James," Caleb said, voice painfully patient, "I will personally switch your exam paper with a blank one if you don't drop this."

James gasped, feigning betrayal. "Wow. Threatening academic sabotage? That's how far you've fallen?"

Caleb rolled his eyes, walking faster. James followed. Caleb slowed down. So did James. At one point, Caleb literally ducked behind a group of students, only for James to pop up on the other side, grinning like a lunatic.

"You cannot escape me, Caleb. Accept it."

"Can I drop out instead?"

"Nope! You have exams to ace."

Speaking of which, their next assessment was already looming—Physics. Caleb took a deep breath, mentally preparing himself. He had conquered his first challenge without getting distracted. Now, all he had to do was survive James' endless teasing and keep his mind clear for the rest of the exams.

Simple, right?

James had been on a mission for days now—to figure out who, exactly, had managed to throw Caleb Miller off his game. It was an anomaly. Caleb was the most focused guy in school, the one who didn't care about anything but grades, formulas, and exams. But something—or someone—had changed that. And James was determined to find out.

"So," James started casually as they walked to their lockers, "this mysterious distraction of yours…"

Caleb sighed. "I don't have a distraction."

James ignored him. "It's gotta be someone from our grade, right?"

"James—"

"Someone smart? You're a nerd, so you'd obviously like someone with at least a few brain cells."

Caleb shook his head, slamming his locker shut. "Drop it."

"Wait—wait—" James snapped his fingers. "Is it someone in our science class? That would explain why you looked like you were mentally solving the Schrödinger equation every time I caught you zoning out."

Caleb clenched his jaw. *This guy is actually insane.*

James gasped dramatically. "Oh my god. Is it one of the seniors? Is that why you're acting weird? You've got a forbidden love situation going on?"

Caleb groaned. "James, I swear, if you don't shut up—"

"You do realize I will be spending every minute of this field trip figuring it out, right?"

"WHAT FIELD TRIP?" asked Caleb , slightly nervous

"oh boy you really don't know anything huh? We are going on a field trip to San Antonio Caleb- San"

Caleb glared at him. "Aight'. so can you focus on the field trip and please not worry about me?"

James smirked. "Nah, I have to worry about you."

Caleb "Well worth a shot, way to go James, way to go"

As the students began boarding the bus for their field trip to San Francisco, Lily was still adjusting to the fact that Sophie had materialized out of nowhere just a day before.

She was about to take a window seat when she heard a familiar voice behind her.

"Well, well, well. Look who finally decided to acknowledge my existence."

Lily turned and saw Sophie grinning at her, arms crossed like she had been waiting for this moment.

Lily gasped. "WHAT ARE YOU EVEN DOING HERE?!"

Sophie laughed. "Uhh, going on the field trip, obviously?" She slid into the seat next to Lily, making herself comfortable. "Did you really think I was gonna let you survive this trip alone?"

Lily groaned. "I forgot you signed up for this! You just vanished for a whole month, and now you pop up like nothing happened?"

Sophie smirked. "I told you—it was all part of my plan. A grand return, dramatic reveal, and now, front-row seats to whatever chaos is about to unfold on this trip."

Lily narrowed her eyes. "You're too entertained by my life."

Sophie shrugged. "Obviously."

Lily sighed.

Sophie raised an eyebrow.

Lily shook her head, looking out the window as the bus started moving. This trip was already off to a chaotic start.

As the bus rolled out of the school gates, Lily leaned back into her seat, finally settling in for the long ride ahead. Sophie, of course, was already making herself way too comfortable—shoes off, earbuds half in, and a bag of snacks appearing out of nowhere.

"Okay," Sophie said between bites of chips, "we've got hours of nothingness ahead. What's the game plan?"

Lily raised an eyebrow. "Game plan?"

Sophie nodded. "Duh. Long bus rides mean maximum gossip, minimal responsibility. So, are we discussing my basketball trip first, or do I get to interrogate you about your mystery life?"

Lily groaned. "I hate that my life is entertainment for you."

Sophie smirked. "That's because it is. But fine, let's start with me." She sat up dramatically. "Picture this: the final match. The scoreboard is tied. There's ten seconds left—"

"Oh great, another Sophie-the-hero story."

"SHH. Let me live my moment." Sophie held up a finger. "As I was saying—ten seconds left. The other team has the ball, but then—bam!—I steal it. Five seconds. I sprint across the court like my life depends on it. Three seconds. I go for the shot. Two. One. The ball's in the air, everyone's watching…"

Lily leaned in. "And?"

Sophie grinned. "And then I missed, obviously."

Lily burst out laughing. "WHAT?! I thought this was a victory story!"

Sophie shrugged. "Nah, but it was dramatic, right?"

Lily shook her head, still laughing. "I swear, you have issues."

Sophie smirked. "Yes, but at least I have good storytelling skills. Now your turn. Anything remotely interesting happen while I was gone?"

Lily hesitated for half a second before saying, "Nope. Nothing."

Sophie squinted at her. "Mmhmm. You hesitated. Suspicious."

Lily rolled her eyes. "You're reading too much into things."

Sophie leaned in, whispering dramatically. "So there is something. Spill."

Before Lily could protest, she noticed James, sitting a few rows ahead, suddenly stretch his arms over his head. As he turned slightly to the side, his gaze casually scanned the bus—until his eyes landed on her.

His entire body froze for a split second. His eyes widened slightly, as if he was not expecting to see her there. And then, just as quickly, he snapped his head forward like he had seen a ghost.

Lily blinked. "…What the- What was that?"

Sophie, who had been too busy digging into her snacks, looked up. "What?"

Lily glanced at James, who was now very aggressively facing the front, looking as if he was trying way too hard to act normal. "…Nothing. Just weird bus energy, I guess."

Sophie shrugged. "Classic school trips. Anyway—where were we?"

Lily, still a little puzzled, shook it off and turned back to her best friend. "You were about to tell me how you embarrassed yourself even more."

Sophie grinned. "Ah, yes. Let's continue."

# 4. Sherlock James and the case of the Invisible crush

As the field trip excitement buzzed through the school, Caleb was doing his best to navigate through the chaos—mainly, dodging James.

James, however, had different plans. He flopped into the seat next to Caleb in the cafeteria, grinning like he had just solved a great mystery. "Alright, I've had enough of this secrecy. Spill it, dude. Who's the lucky person that's got the great Caleb Miller all distracted?"

Caleb nearly choked on his water. "What—James, I told you. There's no one."

James leaned back, folding his arms. "Oh, really? Then why were you spacing out during exams? Why did you suddenly start acting weird whenever certain people walked by?" He squinted. "It's gotta be someone from our grade, right? Or is it an older girl? Oh my god—are you crushing on a senior?"

Caleb facepalmed. "James. Stop."

James ignored him entirely. "Wait, wait, wait… what if it's someone super unexpected? Like—what if it's Ms. Carter from the front office?"

"JAMES!" Caleb hissed, looking around in horror.

James burst out laughing, nearly dropping his sandwich. "Relax, dude! But seriously, I will find out."

Caleb shook his head. "You're wasting your time."

James grinned. "Nah, I'm investing my time. In uncovering the truth." He pointed dramatically. "Mark my words, Caleb Miller. By the end of this field trip, I will know who you like."

Caleb groaned. This trip was going to be exhausting.

James took his mission very seriously. While Caleb tried his best to ignore him, James was quietly gathering evidence, piecing together little clues over the next few days.

Clue #1: The Spacing Out Incident

James first recalled Caleb acting off during their exams. Normally, Caleb was laser-focused, but there were multiple moments when he just... drifted. James had caught him staring into space, deep in thought, pencil frozen mid-air. When James had asked about it, Caleb had brushed it off, but now? Now James knew it had to mean something.

Clue #2: The Cafeteria Slip-Up

A few days before the trip, James had watched as Caleb walked into the cafeteria, grabbed his lunch, and made his way to their usual table—only to suddenly stop, turn around, and go sit somewhere else. Suspicious. Who had he seen? What had made him change course? James had been too far away to tell, but someone had been responsible for that little detour.

Clue #3: The Library Reaction

One day after school, James and Caleb had gone to the library to "study" (mostly James bothering Caleb until he got kicked out). At one point, someone walked past their table, and Caleb had immediately straightened up, looked pretty nervous, adjusted his glasses, and tried way too hard to look casual. Too casual. James had definitely noticed that.

Clue #4: The Mysterious Vanishing Act

Perhaps the most interesting clue was that whoever Caleb had a crush on seemed to be avoiding him—or was Caleb avoiding her? Either way, James had noticed that whenever Caleb entered a room, there was always someone conveniently not there. It was like the universe itself was playing a game of hide-and-seek with his mystery person.

Clue #5: The Almost Confession

James had almost cracked him once. He had jokingly listed a bunch of random names, trying to see if Caleb would react. "Sophia? Emily? Ava? Oh wait, don't tell me—it's Jessica?" Caleb had just rolled his eyes and said, "You're an idiot." But when James had randomly tossed in Lily, there had been a tiny hesitation. A millisecond, but James had caught it.

James' Conclusion

It had taken days of careful observation, deduction, and annoying Caleb to the edge of insanity, but James was almost sure he was onto something.

"Alright," James finally announced, dropping into the seat next to Caleb during lunch. "I have my top suspects."

Caleb sighed. "James, for the last time—"

James held up a hand. "Hear me out. It's either someone from our class who keeps avoiding you or… That girl Lily." He narrowed his eyes. "And I'm betting on Lily."

Caleb froze for half a second before shoving a spoonful of food into his mouth to avoid answering.

James smirked. "I knew it."

Caleb blinked. Once. Twice. His brain struggled to process the fact that James—the same James who once got lost inside the school during a fire drill—had actually figured it out.

He swallowed his food slowly, then cleared his throat. "I have no idea what you're talking about."

James leaned in, his smirk growing. "Ohhh, no, no, no. Don't even try that, Caleb. I saw that reaction. That little micro-expression of terror? You might be good at physics, but you suck at hiding your feelings."

Caleb tried to stay composed. "You're imagining things."

"Am I?" James tilted his head, eyes sparkling with pure mischief. "Let's go over the evidence, shall we? One—you act all weird and spaced out whenever she's around. Two—you physically change direction when she's nearby. Three—you got all awkward that one time in the library, and don't even get me started on the way you just froze when I mentioned her name."

Caleb sighed, pinching the bridge of his nose. "James—"

"And finally," James continued, completely ignoring him, "we've got the most important question of all." He wiggled his eyebrows and grinned.

Caleb already knew he was going to regret asking. "...What?"

James leaned in dramatically, voice dropping to a whisper. "You're gonna confess to her, right?"

Caleb choked on his water. "WHAT?!"

James laughed so hard he nearly fell off his chair. "Dude! That was the loudest reaction yet! I GOT YOU!"

Caleb groaned, rubbing his face. "James. No. I am not confessing anything. It's not even that big of a deal."

James gasped, clutching his chest. "Not a big deal?! Caleb, my man, my genius, this is your chance! A whole field trip? Hours of bonding time? Long, dramatic moments where you two could accidentally get paired together? And you are gonna waste it by not confessing?!"

Caleb shook his head firmly. "It's not happening. It's just a small, meaningless—"

James pointed at him. "You can keep lying to yourself, but I know the truth."

Caleb shook his head furiously. "James, I don't even talk to her. I barely know her. There is no way I'm confessing anything."

James squinted at him like he had just said the dumbest thing in the world. "Okay, hold on. Let me get this straight. You like her."

"I barely like her," Caleb corrected.

James ignored him. "But you've never actually spoken to her?"

Caleb crossed his arms. "No."

James blinked. "Not even a 'Hey, can I borrow a pen?' or a 'Move, you're blocking the board'?"

Caleb sighed. "Nope."

James gasped dramatically. "BRO. You've got a crush on a complete stranger?"

Caleb groaned. "It's not a crush—it's just… I don't know. A small, temporary thing that will go away if you stop talking about it."

James grinned. "Oh, you poor, clueless nerd. Do you even know anything about her?"

Caleb hesitated. "She's… in our grade?"

James stared at him. "Wow. The love is thriving."

"Shut up," Caleb muttered.

James sighed, shaking his head like he was disappointed in humanity. "Alright, this is worse than I thought. Not only are you not going to confess, but you don't even have a basic friendship to work with."

"Exactly." Caleb nodded. "So, drop it."

James, of course, did not drop it. Instead, he leaned back, smirking. "You know what this means, right?"

Caleb narrowed his eyes. "What?"

James grinned. "We've got a whole field trip to fix this."

# 5. Unplanned Chaos

The field trip was already a disaster, at least for Caleb. Between James' endless teasing and the unfortunate fact that Lily seemed completely unaware of his existence, he was ready to vanish into the void.

But fate—and their teacher—had other plans.

The bus rumbled down the highway, the excitement buzzing as they neared San Antonio.

"Alright, everyone, listen up!" "We'll be stopping for a short break before heading into the city. Stretch your legs, grab some snacks, and most importantly—do not cause chaos."their teacher announced as students boarded the bus. "Also,since some of you are way too loud , we're switching up seats."

Groans echoed through the bus. Caleb sighed. Whatever. Just let me sit with James.

"Caleb, you'll be sitting with—"

Please, please, please be James.

"—Lily."

Caleb's stomach dropped. James choked on air.

Lily, who had been settling into her usual seat with Sophie, froze.

"What?" she blurted.

Sophie gasped. "What?"

James fist-pumped. "YES."

Lily turned to their teacher. "Um, sorry, but Lily and I sit together. That's our thing."

"Yeah," Lily added quickly. "Tradition."

The teacher crossed her arms. "New traditions, then. Sit down."

Sophie looked outraged. "This is a violation of friendship law!"

"Nothing I can do," their teacher said, already moving to the next row.

Lily let out a dramatic sigh before sliding into the seat next to Caleb, stiff as a board. Caleb, now shifting to the window seat,equally horrified, focused on the window like his life depended on it.

Meanwhile, right behind Caleb and Lily, Sophie and James were now forced to sit next to each other.

Sophie frowned. "I don't want talk to you."

James grinned. "Perfect! Neither do I."

Caleb groaned. This trip was going to be so long.

Twenty minutes into the ride, Caleb reached for his water bottle just as Lily did.

Their hands collided.

Both of them froze.

The bottle slipped, rolling right into Sophie's bag.

Sophie scowled. "Seriously?"

James, having the time of his life, smirked. "Wow. True love in action."

Lily groaned, shoving the bottle back at Caleb. "This doesn't mean anything."

Caleb, still internally combusting, muttered, "Right. Yep. Just physics."

James wiggled his eyebrows. "Physics? You mean, like… attraction?"

Lily turned to glare at him. "Say one more word and I'm throwing you off this bus."

Sophie sighed dramatically. "I am stuck next to this idiot for hours, aren't I?"

James beamed. "Buckle up, Soph. We're in this together now."

Sophie fake-gagged. "SOPH?? and I'd rather walk."

At their first stop, everyone lined up for lunch in the cafeteria. Caleb was trying very hard to avoid James, but Lily was ahead of them, ordering food.

James leaned in. "Bet you won't say anything to her right now."

Caleb glared. "What am I even supposed to say? 'Hey, you order food like a pro'?"

Before James could push him into total humiliation, Lily turned—holding her tray, not looking where she was going.

She walked straight into Caleb.

The next three seconds were pure chaos.

Her drink tipped. The tray wobbled. Caleb, in an attempt to save it, grabbed onto the wrong thing—Lily's wrist instead of the tray.

Gravity did its job.

The tray crashed. The drink spilled. And now?

Caleb had chili fries all over his shirt.

Lily gasped. "Oh my God!"

Caleb looked down at himself. Then at her.

James lost it. "OH NO. NOT THE CHILI FRIES. ANYTHING BUT THE CHILI FRIES."

Lily frantically grabbed napkins. "I'm so sorry! Here, let me—"

She started dabbing at his shirt, which somehow made it worse. Caleb was too stunned to function.

The entire cafeteria was watching.

Sophie sighed. "Before Lily accidentally strangles him with napkins, let's just—" She shoved a water bottle into Caleb's hand.

Lily groaned. "I swear, I'll pay for your lunch—"

Caleb, still recovering, muttered, "Uh. It's fine."

James wiped away fake tears. "Man, what are the odds that the one person who spills food on you is your secret crush?"

Caleb kicked him under the table.

Later that day, the group visited a suspension bridge over a river. The wooden planks creaked with every step.

James was thrilled. Caleb? Not so much.

"This is easy," Sophie scoffed. "It's just a bridge."

 Lily gave her a thumbs-up. "Right."

Caleb leaned against the metal railing, his gaze fixed on the river far below. The water shimmered under the midday sun, moving lazily beneath the suspension bridge. It was quiet here, except for the occasional creak of the cables swaying in the breeze.

James stood beside him, hands in his pockets, scanning the horizon. "It's kind of peaceful up here, isn't it?"

Caleb exhaled, his fingers tapping idly against the metal. "Yeah. Like the world slows down for a second."

James smirked. "Or maybe you're just lost in thought. Thinking about her again?"

Caleb turned slightly, but there was no point in denying it. "Maybe." He sighed. "I can't help it, man. She's always there. In my head."

James chuckled. "Have you even talked to her yet?"

Caleb shook his head. "No. Every time I think about it, something gets in the way."

James clapped him on the shoulder. "You'll get your chance. Maybe today's the day."

Caleb hesitated, then looked at his friend. "Maybe. What about you? Saw you glancing sophie!"

James gave a half-shrug, like it wasn't something he'd seriously considered. "Whatever dude"

Caleb grinned. "yeah sure sure"

A few steps away, Lily and Sophie approached the bridge, laughing about something neither Caleb nor James could hear. Caleb's fingers tensed against the railing. Maybe today really was the day.

Lily stood at the edge of the suspension bridge, gripping the worn wooden railing. The planks beneath her feet creaked as the wind whistled through the cables, making the entire structure sway ever so slightly. She swallowed hard, her heart pounding in her chest.

Ahead, Sophie was already on the other side, waiting with an easy smile. "Come on, Lil! It's not that bad!" she called, her voice carrying over the gap between them.

Lily exhaled, steadying herself. It wasn't that she was afraid of heights—at least, that's what she kept telling herself. But there was something unnerving about the way the bridge shifted under every step, like it wasn't meant to hold too much weight at once.

Behind her, footsteps echoed against the planks. She turned her head slightly. Caleb and James had just stepped onto the bridge, moving at a steady pace, the ropes bouncing ever so slightly under their weight.

Caleb's gaze flickered toward her, just for a second, before he looked ahead again.

No turning back now.

Lily took a breath and stepped forward. The wood groaned beneath her, and instinctively, she tightened her grip on the railing. Another step. And another. The ropes creaked with the wind, the bridge shifting with every movement.

She focused on Sophie, who was still waiting, still smiling. "You got this!" Sophie encouraged.

Lily nodded, more to herself than anyone else, and kept walking.

Behind her, Caleb and James moved forward as well, their presence somehow both unnoticed and entirely impossible to ignore.


Lily walked forward, steady, focused. The suspension bridge swayed slightly beneath her, but she ignored it. Sophie was already on the other side, waiting with a raised eyebrow, as if to say, Hurry up.

She stepped forward again—

And then—

CRACK.

The wooden plank beneath her foot snapped.

Her stomach lurched as her foot plunged downward. She gasped, arms flailing, balance gone—

And then—

A hand clamped around her wrist.

Tight. Steady.

The sudden force yanked her back onto solid planks. Her breath was stuck in her throat as she braced herself, her fingers gripping onto—a hoodie sleeve?

She blinked. Looked up.

Caleb.

For a second, neither of them moved. His grip on her wrist was firm, his eyes wide—not just startled, but genuinely concerned. His other hand had instinctively grabbed the rope railing, his knuckles white.

Lily's heart was still hammering, but not just from the fall anymore. She realized she was holding onto his sleeve.

She let go immediately.

"Uh," she muttered, stepping back. "Thanks."

Caleb blinked like he had just processed what happened. His grip on her wrist loosened, and he pulled his hand away. "Yeah. Sure." His voice was quiet. Maybe uncertain.

Behind them, James let out a sharp breath.

"Wait—wait. Did that just happen?" His voice was somewhere between shock and amusement. "Did you just—bro, you saved her."

Lily turned her head slightly, but not enough to make eye contact.

James, clearly not picking up on the awkwardness, leaned toward Caleb and loudly whispered, "She totally liked that."

Lily shot him a glare. "I can hear you."

James immediately straightened, looking away as if he hadn't said anything. Caleb pressed his lips together, exhaling through his nose.

From the other side of the bridge, Sophie, who had been watching the entire thing, crossed her arms. "Are you guys coming or what?"

Lily nodded stiffly and moved forward, more cautious this time. Caleb followed, hands shoved in his hoodie pocket, saying nothing. James trailed after them, still processing what had just happened.

And when they finally reached the other side, Lily could still feel it—

The way Caleb had grabbed her wrist. The way his expression had looked almost worried. The way things suddenly felt... different.

And yet, none of them had ever really spoken before.

That, she realized, was about to change.

Lily stepped off the last plank and onto solid ground, exhaling like she had just finished an Olympic sprint. The bridge was behind her. She was fine. She was totally fine.

...Except for the fact that her entire face was burning.

She refused to turn around, but she knew Caleb was still right behind her. He hadn't said a word, but she could feel him there, standing just a few centimeters away, probably checking if she was okay.

James, of course, had no such sense of subtlety.

He strutted past Caleb and threw his arms in the air. "AND THEY MADE IT, FOLKS! WHAT A HEROIC RESCUE! WHAT A STUNNING DISPLAY OF BRIDGE-CROSSING ABILITY!"

Lily shot him a look. "Are you done?"

Sophie, however, was looking at Lily a little too closely. Then—her lips curled into a smirk.

"Lily," she said slowly, eyes twinkling. "Your face is so red."

Lily stiffened. "It's not—"

"Oh my god, are you BLUSHING?" Sophie grinned like she had just uncovered the juiciest secret. "Is it because Caleb—"

"I ALMOST FELL TO MY DEATH." Lily's voice cracked as she waved her arms dramatically. "Maybe it's because of that, Sophie."

"Uh-huh." Sophie wiggled her eyebrows. "Or maybe—"

"Sophie," Lily deadpanned. "Stop."

Sophie did not stop. In fact, she turned to Caleb, who was now standing there looking like he wanted the ground to swallow him. "Hey, Caleb, what do you think? Is her face—"

Caleb immediately looked anywhere except at Lily. "I—uh—I don't know?" His voice came out awkwardly high-pitched, and James lost it.

"My guy is so nervous right now," James wheezed. "Bro, you literally held her hand. This is, like, the first step to marriage."

Caleb groaned. "James, I swear—"

Lily groaned louder. "I'M LEAVING."

And with that, she stomped off, Sophie cackling beside her. Caleb rubbed his face like he was regretting every life choice that led him here, while James patted his back proudly.

Over the next few days, things between them weren't exactly the same as before.

For one, they actually talked now.

Somehow, without really planning it, the four of them kept ending up together. They wandered through the historic streets of San Antonio, stopping by the Alamo, pretending to be experts on history.

They took pictures by the River Walk, where James nearly fell into the water while trying to impress no one in particular. They got food at a random taco truck, where Sophie made fun of Lily for getting mild salsa like a coward.

It was… fun.

And then came the fireworks.

That night, none of them had expected anything. They had just been walking along the quiet streets, full from a late-night snack run, when suddenly—

BOOM.

A burst of color lit up the sky.

Lily startled slightly at the first explosion, then looked up as the sky erupted into gold, red, and blue sparks. People on the street cheered, but she barely noticed them.

It was just fireworks. Nothing special. But for some reason, she couldn't stop staring.

Caleb saw her before he saw the fireworks.

She was a few steps ahead of him, eyes wide, face glowing in the flickering light. And for the first time since they met, he saw her completely unguarded—just watching, just smiling, like a little kid seeing something magical for the first time.

He swallowed. Looked away.

James elbowed him. "Dude. DUDE."

Caleb didn't respond.

James grinned. "You're so done."

Sophie, standing next to Lily, caught the way Caleb kept glancing over. She leaned toward Lily and whispered, "Your face is getting red again."

Lily groaned. "STOP."

But Sophie just smirked, and James kept laughing, and above them, the fireworks kept bursting—colorful and endless, like something out of a dream.

And somehow, in that moment, everything felt different.

And maybe—just maybe—this is love.

The bus rumbled softly beneath them, its gentle vibrations making the long journey back to Maplewood High feel strangely soothing. The once-lively energy of their trip had quieted, replaced by a calm exhaustion.

Lily sat beside Caleb.

At first, she didn't think much of it. They had spent the past few days hanging out—kind of by accident, kind of not—and sitting next to him felt almost… normal now. But after the first hour of silence, something shifted.

She glanced at Caleb.

He was leaning back, one earbud in, lazily scrolling through his phone. He looked so *at ease?*, like sitting next to her wasn't a big deal at all. Meanwhile, she felt—what? Awkward? Was she *overthinking* this?

Yeah. Probably.

Determined to make things feel normal again, she cleared her throat. "So… was that whole saving-me thing pre-planned, or are you just naturally that heroic?"

Caleb turned his head slightly, a slow smirk pulling at his lips. "Oh, totally pre-planned. Had it all mapped out. Just waited for you to step on the wrong plank."

Lily rolled her eyes. "Right, because letting me *almost die* is such a genius plan."

Caleb chuckled. "I mean, if you *really* think about it, I made the moment way more cinematic."

Lily let out a dramatic gasp. "*You* made it cinematic? I was the one who nearly fell to my doom! Where's *my* credit?"

Caleb tapped his chin, pretending to think. "Okay, fine. You played your part well."

She shot him a playful glare. "Gee, thanks."

The conversation flowed effortlessly after that. They laughed about James' *near-death* experience with the river, how Sophie forced Lily to eat spicy salsa (*and then cackled as she suffered*), and even their favorite places from the trip. Lily gushed about how cool the Alamo was, while Caleb casually admitted that he wasn't *really* into history.

Lily gasped in mock offense. "Wow. *Wow.* I cannot believe you."

Caleb raised an eyebrow. "You spent twenty minutes staring at a shelf full of gift shop magnets."

"They were *tiny* historical figures, Caleb. That's *art.*"

Caleb huffed a laugh and shook his head, but there was something soft in his eyes when he looked at her—something he didn't really bother to hide anymore.

Then, out of nowhere, Lily asked, "So… what do you wanna do after high school?"

Caleb blinked, caught off guard by the sudden shift. "Like, career-wise?"

"Yeah," Lily said, tilting her head. "You seem like a *you'll-figure-it-out-later* type of guy."

Caleb smirked. "Ouch."

Lily grinned. "Am I wrong?"

He chuckled, shaking his head. "Nah. But actually, I kinda do have a plan."

Lily raised an eyebrow. "Oh?"

Caleb hesitated for half a second, then shrugged. "I wanna make music. Maybe start a boy band."

Lily blinked. That was… unexpected. "Wait, really?"

"Yeah." Caleb rubbed the back of his neck, looking almost *shy* for the first time. "I mean, I love singing. Been writing some songs, messing around with some beats. I just think it'd be cool, you know? Making something real. Something people can *feel*."

Lily was quiet for a second.

Then she smiled. "That's actually *really* cool."

Caleb glanced at her. "You think?"

"Yeah. You should do it."

Caleb looked away, but there was something soft in his expression. "Thanks," he said, quieter than before.

And just like that, the conversation shifted again. They kept talking, kept laughing. But soon, the bus grew quieter. The road stretched endlessly ahead of them, the streetlights outside flickering past in rhythmic intervals.

Lily yawned.

Caleb glanced at her just in time to see her lean against the window, blinking slowly, her exhaustion finally catching up to her.

A few minutes later, she was asleep.

And Caleb?

He was *done for.*

Because—god. She was adorable.

Her breathing was soft and even, her lips slightly parted as she nestled into the corner of the seat. A few strands of hair had fallen over her face, and Caleb had to physically stop himself from reaching out to brush them back.

Instead, he just stared for a second longer than necessary.

Then he noticed the slight way she curled into herself, her arms tucked close like she was cold.

Without thinking, he peeled off his hoodie. He hesitated for a moment, just long enough to talk himself out of it—except he *didn't* talk himself out of it.

Carefully—*so* carefully—he draped it over her shoulders, making sure it covered her completely.

She stirred slightly but didn't wake.

Caleb exhaled, relaxing back into his seat.

Then—

A snort.

Caleb closed his eyes. *Oh no.*

James.

James and Sophie, who had been sitting behind them. *Watching.*

James, who was *grinning like an idiot.*

Caleb sighed. "Don't."

James bit his lip like he was trying not to explode. "I didn't say anything."

"Don't *think* anything either."

James wiggled his eyebrows. "Too late."

Caleb groaned, dragging a hand down his face.

But as he sat there, pretending to be annoyed, his gaze flickered back to Lily—still curled up, still fast asleep, his hoodie drowning her frame.

And suddenly, he didn't really mind James' teasing at all.

# 6. Something Feels…Off

Lily knew something was *wrong* the moment she stepped into Maplewood High.

Everything *looked* normal—the hallways buzzing with the usual morning chaos, students scrambling to finish homework, and James loudly arguing about the *moon landing being fake*.

But there was something in the air. A tension she couldn't quite place. Like the universe was winding up, waiting to *snap*.

And then—

It did.

The fire alarm *shrieked* through the school.

Students *froze*.

Then—pure *chaos*.

Lockers slammed. Papers flew. Someone tripped over their own backpack.

And then—

**Caleb.**

Storming out of the science lab, face covered in *black soot*.

James was *right behind him*, equally soot-covered, his *entire backpack smoking*.

For a second, Lily's brain just... *stalled.*

Then James *whisper-yelled,* "RUN."


**Five minutes earlier**

Caleb *knew* this was a terrible idea.

He stood in the science lab, watching James hold up something *very questionable.*

James grinned. "Okay, but like… what if we just *see* what happens?"

Caleb sighed. "Dude."

James wiggled his eyebrows. "Think about it. This could be *scientific discovery.*"

"This is *detention* waiting to happen."

Before Caleb could stop him, James *shoved the object inside the microwave* and hit *START.*

The moment the microwave hummed to life, Caleb felt *fear.*

A horrifying *crackle* filled the air. Sparks. The microwave *shook.*

Then—

*BOOM.*

Black *smoke* exploded out. Caleb stumbled backward, coughing as soot *coated* his face.

James blinked at the wreckage. Then at Caleb.

"…Maybe we should—"

*FIRE ALARM.*

James grabbed his backpack. "*RUN.*"


Lily watched, *horrified*, as Caleb and James *sprinted* down the hall.

"WHAT DID YOU *DO?!*" she shouted.

Caleb barely glanced back, his voice *way* too casual for someone *actively fleeing a crime scene.* "*I CAN EXPLAIN!*"

Behind them, the science teacher stormed out of the lab, *fuming.*

"WHO PUT METAL IN THE MICROWAVE?!"

Lily's jaw *dropped.*

Across the hallway, Sophie casually took a sip of her iced coffee, completely unbothered.

Lily turned to her. "Are you seeing this?"

Sophie nodded. "Mhm." Another sip. "Should we be worried?"

Lily watched as Caleb and James disappeared around the corner.

She exhaled.

"Sophie, I think today's about to be *very* weird."

he school parking lot was *chaos.*

Students were *everywhere,* buzzing with excitement over the *unexpected half-day.* Some were celebrating, others were still trying to figure out *what the heck just happened.*

And in the middle of it all—

Lily.

Standing in front of Caleb, arms crossed, eyes narrowed.

"…Okay," she said slowly. "Explain."

Caleb, still slightly covered in soot, sighed. "It's… complicated."

"*Complicated? Caleb.* You and James just shut down *the entire school.*"

James, standing behind Caleb, beamed. "Not to brag, but yeah. Pretty legendary."

Lily ignored him. "So what *exactly* did you do?"

Caleb hesitated. Then, rubbing the back of his neck, he muttered, "…We may have microwaved something that shouldn't be microwaved."

Lily *gasped*. "You IDIOTS. You *actually* did the thing that every school warns you *not* to do?!"

"In our defense," James chimed in, "we didn't *know* it would explode that badly."

Sophie, who had been standing quietly this whole time, finally spoke up. "…What *was* it?"

James and Caleb exchanged a glance.

"…Aluminum foil," Caleb admitted.

Lily *gasped again*, dramatically clutching her chest. "THE CLICHÉ! YOU GUYS DID *THE MOST OBVIOUSLY DUMB THING POSSIBLE?!*"

James threw his hands in the air. "I was doing *an experiment!*"

"Oh, wow, what a *brilliant* scientist you are, James. Maybe next time try *not setting the school on fire?*"

Caleb sighed. "Look, we didn't *mean* to—"

"I hope it was *worth* it, because now you two have *detention* for a week."

James groaned. "Not fair. That fire alarm was *way* too sensitive. It was barely a *mini explosion.*"

"James," Sophie deadpanned, "your *backpack was smoking.*"

James blinked. "Yeah, but like, just a little."

Lily threw her hands up. "I *cannot* with you two."

And with that, she walked toward her bike.

The air was *crisp* as they rode through the quiet streets, the unexpected half-day making everything feel a little *lighter.*

Lily pedaled alongside Caleb, the two of them falling into an easy rhythm as James and Sophie rode a bit ahead, still arguing over whether or not this incident would make it into the *school newspaper.*

For a few minutes, neither Lily nor Caleb spoke. Just the sound of their tires against the pavement, the occasional wind sweeping past them.

Then—

"…So," Caleb finally said, glancing at her, "you *really* think I'm an idiot, huh?"

Lily smirked. "Oh, *absolutely.*"

Caleb chuckled, shaking his head. "Not even a little credit for saving you on that bridge?"

She pretended to think. "Mmm… alright. I *guess* you get some points for that."

Caleb grinned. "Wow, so generous."

Lily rolled her eyes but smiled.

For a while, they just rode in comfortable silence again. The sun was warm on their backs, the world quiet except for the occasional rustling of leaves.

Then, *completely out of nowhere*, Lily's bike wobbled.

"Whoa—" she yelped, trying to steady herself.

Before she could tip over, Caleb instinctively reached out, grabbing the handlebar of her bike. His fingers brushed against hers for half a second before she got control again.

They both froze.

"…You good?" Caleb asked, still holding onto her bike for a moment longer than necessary.

Lily swallowed. "Uh. Yeah. Just hit a weird bump."

He let go, but the way he looked at her—just for a second—made her heart *do a weird thing*.

Lily cleared her throat, looking straight ahead. "You know, if you're gonna be my personal safety net, at least try not to *blow up the school* next time."

Caleb smirked. "No promises."

Lily groaned. "Oh my *god*."

And as they rode down the quiet streets, the sun dipping lower in the sky, Caleb glanced at her again—

And smiled.

Sophie had seen this coming from a *mile* away.

It wasn't even subtle.

From the moment Caleb *dramatically* saved Lily on that bridge to the *ridiculous* hoodie moment on the bus (*seriously, could he be more obvious?*), Sophie knew.

And now? After the bike ride, after the way Caleb had *literally grabbed Lily's handlebar like some rom-com lead?*

Yeah. It was time to make things *happen*.

She glanced at James, who was casually riding beside her, and smirked. "We *have* to do something."

James barely hesitated. "Oh, *100%*."

Because behind them? Caleb and Lily were *so painfully obvious*.

Lily, pretending like she *wasn't* still flustered from that whole *"oh no, my bike is wobbling, oh no, Caleb just saved me again"* moment.
Caleb, pretending like he *hadn't* instinctively reached for her.
And now? The two of them were *extra careful* not to look at each other, which was *so much worse*.

James snorted. "Dude. They are *screaming* 'we like each other' without even realizing it."

Sophie grinned. "Exactly. Which is why it's our duty—*as their wonderful, supportive friends*—to *push* them in the right direction."

James stroked his chin dramatically. "Agreed. But we gotta be *smooth* about it."

Sophie nodded. "They can't know it's us."

James' eyes lit up. "Secret matchmaking mission?"

Sophie smirked. "Secret matchmaking mission."

James held out his fist. Sophie bumped it. *It was on.*


They slowed their pace *just enough* for Caleb and Lily to catch up. Then—right as the two *unsuspecting victims* pulled alongside them—James turned, *grinning.*

"So…" he said, drawing out the word. "You guys look *awfully* cozy back there."

Lily immediately groaned. "James, *no.*"

Caleb sighed. "James, *please.*"

Sophie placed a hand over her heart. "Oh, don't be shy, you *two.*" She batted her eyelashes. "First, he saves your *life,* and *now* he's catching you on your bike? That's *literally* fate."

Lily *nearly* swerved off the road.

James gasped dramatically. "Ohhh wowww"

Lily's face turned *so red,* Sophie almost *felt* bad. Almost.

Caleb groaned. "You *both* need new hobbies."

"Oh, *this* is our hobby now," Sophie said sweetly.

James grinned. "And we are *fully committed* to the cause."

Lily muttered something under her breath that sounded suspiciously like *"I hate you both"*, while Caleb just let out the *biggest* sigh of his life.

But neither of them denied anything.

And Sophie and James?

They just exchanged a *victorious* look.

Because *Operation: Set Them Up?*

Was *officially* in motion.

# 7. "The Setup"

What a week huh? It's already Friday night

Sophie sat cross-legged on her bed, phone pressed to her ear, a *devious* smirk forming on her lips.

"So, what are you doing this weekend?" she asked casually.

On the other end, Lily sighed. "Probably catching up on sleep after surviving another week of *James and Caleb's nonsense.*"

Sophie rolled her eyes. "Well, I have *better* plans for you. We're going to the arcade and bowling alley tomorrow."

Lily blinked. "…We *are?*"

"Yup."

Lily hesitated. "Is this another one of your *schemes?*"

Sophie gasped dramatically. "Lily, please. Would I *ever*—"

"Yes."

"…Fair. But no, this is just a *fun* little hangout. Me and you."

Lily frowned. "Wait. Just us two?"

"Uh-huh," Sophie said smoothly. "It'll be *super chill.*"

On the other end of the city, James was making a *very* similar call.

---

**Caleb's Room – Friday Night**

Caleb was lying on his bed, lazily scrolling through his phone when it *buzzed* with an incoming call from James.

"Dude," James said the second Caleb picked up. "Wanna hit up the arcade and bowling alley tomorrow?"

Caleb frowned. "I guess? Who's going?"

"Just me and you."

Caleb raised an eyebrow. "That's it?"

"Yup. No surprises. No hidden agendas."

Caleb sat up. "…This feels suspicious."

James gasped. "Me? Suspicious? *How dare you?*"

Caleb narrowed his eyes. "Are you *lying* to me right now?"

"Would I *ever* lie to you?"

"Yes."

"…Okay, but still. Just come. It'll be fun."

After a long pause, Caleb sighed. "Fine."

James grinned. *Step one: success.*

**The Hangout (a.k.a. The Setup, Phase Two)**

The next day, Lily and Caleb arrived at the arcade **at the exact same time**—only to freeze in place when they saw each other.

Caleb blinked. "Wait. *You're here?*"

Lily's eyes narrowed. "You are *also* here?"

And then—

"Oops," Sophie said *way* too innocently.

James coughed. "Our bad. Did we *forget* to mention each other was coming?"

Lily glared at Sophie. "I *knew* you were up to something."

Caleb shot James a look. "You *set us up.*"

James grinned. "Yup."

Sophie nudged Lily. "Well, since you *both* showed up anyway… might as well stay, right?"

Lily groaned. "You *two* are the worst."

Caleb sighed. "Fine. But *if* this turns out to be some elaborate plan, just know—I *will* get revenge."

James snorted. "Bro, if this *was* a plan, wouldn't we be, like… watching your every move and taking notes on how cute you two are together?"

Sophie grinned. "Which we *totally* wouldn't do."

Caleb and Lily exchanged a look.

Lily sighed. "Whatever. Let's just play."

---

**Phase One: Bowling Disaster**

Things went *south* almost immediately.

Lily was, quite frankly, **the worst bowler in existence**.

Her first throw? The ball *rolled into the next lane*, knocking over *someone else's* pins.

James *collapsed* from laughter. "SHE STOLE SOMEONE ELSE'S STRIKE."

Lily covered her face. "I want to *disappear.*"

Meanwhile, Caleb was *trying* (and failing) not to laugh. "Do you, uh… want help?"

Lily *glared.* "Like you're any better."

Caleb picked up a ball, rolled it down the lane, and—
**strike.**

Lily's jaw *dropped.*

James fist-bumped the air. "Bro. That was *hot.*"

Lily, flustered for *some reason*, picked up another ball. "Fine. I got this."

She did *not* have this.

It *immediately* went into the gutter.

Sophie *cackled*. "Incredible. The form. The technique."

Caleb smirked. "Still think I need help?"

Lily sighed. "…Fine."

Caleb casually walked up behind her, adjusting her stance, his hands lightly brushing her arms. "Try aiming this way," he murmured.

Lily *froze*.

Why was he *so close?*

She quickly stepped forward. "YEP. OKAY. I GOT IT. THANKS."

Sophie and James exchanged a victorious glance. *Oh yeah. This was working.*


After *barely* surviving bowling, they moved to the arcade.

That's when disaster struck.

Lily, distracted while checking her phone, *accidentally bumped into someone.*

*A very cute someone?*

The guy—tall, messy hair, charming smile—turned around. "Woah, hey. You okay?"

Lily quickly nodded. "Yeah! Sorry about that."

He chuckled. "No problem. I'm Kevin, by the way."

Caleb, standing *right next to her*, **immediately disliked this guy.**

Kevin glanced at the claw machine Lily had been eyeing. "Trying to win something?"

"Oh, yeah," she said. "But these are *totally rigged.*"

Kevin smirked. "Want me to give it a shot?"

Before Lily could answer, Caleb *stepped in front of her.*

"*Actually,*" Caleb said *way* too smoothly, "I *already* won her something."

And then, **like an absolute menace**, Caleb pulled out the **giant plushie bear** he had won earlier.

Lily's eyes widened. "…Wait. When did you—"

Caleb smirked. "I guess I'm just good at winning."

Kevin blinked. "Oh. Cool, man."

Lily, flustered *again*, took the bear. "Uh… thanks?"

Jake, clearly getting the message, smiled politely and walked off.

James *stared* at Caleb.

Sophie *stared* at Caleb.

Then—

James burst out laughing. "BRO. YOU JUST *ALPHA-MOVED* THAT GUY."

Sophie wiped fake tears. "Caleb, *sweetie*, just say you were jealous."

Caleb scoffed. "I *wasn't* jealous."

James grinned. "Dude, you literally *whipped out a giant teddy bear* like it was a declaration of war."

Lily, hugging the bear, mumbled, "It was kinda impressive."

Caleb smirked. "Told you I was good at winning."

Sophie gasped. "Lily. You're *so gone* for him."

James grinned. "And he's *so gone* for her."

Lily groaned. "I *hate* you both."

Sophie and James just high-fived.

Because *Operation: Set Them Up*?

Was going *even better* than expected.

# 8.Detention, Distraction & Dumb Feelings

Caleb should have known this day would be *a disaster* the second he walked into school.

Maybe it was the way James was already smirking when he saw him. Maybe it was the way Sophie *wouldn't stop staring at him* during homeroom.

Or maybe—just *maybe*—it was the fact that, by lunchtime, Caleb was sitting in **detention**.

With **James.**

And **Lily.**

And **Sophie.**

Because of course, if Caleb was suffering, the universe had to make it **a group experience.**

**Flashback**

It started with James. Because *obviously* it did.

Technically, Caleb and James were **already sentenced to detention** for the whole *microwave explosion* incident.

But Lily and Sophie?

68

**That was a work of fate.**

During lunch, Lily and Sophie were *minding their own business*, discussing how **dumb Caleb and James were**, when—

A **food fight** broke out.

And guess who got **hit in the crossfire?**

**Lily.**

With an **entire** carton of chocolate milk.

Direct. Hit.

Sophie *screamed.* "MY BEST FRIEND HAS BEEN *ATTACKED.*"

Lily, dripping chocolate milk, stood up *so fast*, she knocked over an entire lunch tray.

Which—of course—fell directly onto a **teacher's shoes.**

**Five minutes later, detention.**

**Present: Detention. Or, the Worst Place on Earth.**


Lily sat with her arms crossed, still faintly smelling like chocolate milk, glaring at James.

"This is your fault."

James raised an eyebrow. "*My* fault? How is the food fight **my** fault?"

"Because," Lily said, "chaos follows you like a **lost puppy.**"

Caleb smirked. "She's not wrong."

James scoffed. "You know what? Maybe detention is *good* for you guys. Maybe you should *reflect* on your terrible attitudes."

Sophie fake-gasped. "Is James suggesting *self-improvement*? I need to write this down."

James rolled his eyes. "You're all so dramatic."

The detention supervisor, an old teacher who looked **one coffee away from retirement**, stood at the front, flipping through a newspaper. He barely even *acknowledged* them.

Which was a mistake.

Because **James and Sophie were about to make things worse.**


After **ten whole minutes** of silence, James got bored.

And when James got bored, **bad things happened.**

He leaned over his desk and whispered, "Let's play *Truth or Dare*."

Lily *glared*. "Are you trying to get us all in more trouble?"

James smirked. "I would *never*."

Sophie gasped dramatically. "Oh, no. *Lily's scared.*"

Lily rolled her eyes. "I'm not scared."

Caleb, watching this unfold, sighed. "I already hate this."

James *grinned*. "Too late. It's happening."

And so began **the worst game of Truth or Dare in detention history.**

Sophie went first. "Lily. Truth or Dare?"

Lily groaned. "Truth."

Sophie smirked. "Okay. **Do you think Caleb is cute?**"

Lily *choked*.

Caleb **straightened immediately**.

James *wheezed*.

The detention room **suddenly felt too small**.

Lily's face turned bright red. "I—I—WHAT KIND OF QUESTION—"

"You picked *Truth*," Sophie said innocently.

Lily *glared* at her best friend, then *very aggressively* muttered, **"Fine. Yes. Whatever."**

Caleb blinked.

Sophie's *smirk* grew. "Oh? **Yes, what?**"

Lily avoided eye contact. "Yes, okay? He's *objectively* good-looking. Are you *happy now?*"

James grinned at Caleb. "Dude. You're **objectively** hot. How does it feel?"

Caleb, who had *zero* clue what to do with this information, cleared his throat and muttered, "Uh. Cool. Thanks?"

Lily wanted to **disappear.**

Sophie and James wanted to **high-five.**

This was **going better than expected.**

And detention?

Suddenly, **not so boring anymore.**


Lily regretted *everything.*

She regretted picking **Truth**.
She regretted **answering honestly**.
And most of all—she regretted the way Caleb was now *casually existing* next to her like she hadn't just admitted he was **objectively good-looking.**

Because now?

James and Sophie were on a **mission.**

Lily *could feel it.*

James was grinning **way too much**. Sophie kept looking between her and Caleb like she was *mentally writing their wedding vows.*

Meanwhile, Caleb?

Completely unreadable.

Which was **annoying**. Because she had just *embarrassed herself in front of him*, and he had the *audacity* to just… sit there? Looking **annoyingly cute and unbothered?**

Lily *hated* this.

"Alright, my turn," Caleb suddenly said, leaning back in his chair.

Lily froze. *Oh no.*

His gaze flickered to James.

"Truth or Dare?" Caleb asked.

James grinned. "Dare."

Caleb smirked. "Great. I dare you to *shut up for the rest of detention.*"

Sophie *gasped.*

Lily's eyes widened.

James *looked horrified.* "BRO. WHAT."

Caleb shrugged. "You picked *Dare.*"

James opened his mouth. Closed it. Opened it *again.* Then let out the most **dramatic sigh in existence** before slumping in his chair, defeated.

Sophie wiped away a fake tear. "Rest in peace, James' ability to speak. Gone but not forgotten."

Lily, still flustered from *everything*, muttered, "Finally, some peace and quiet."

James *silently flipped her off.*

Sophie *cackled.*

Caleb just smirked.

And somehow, detention *actually* felt a little fun.




About **twenty minutes later**, detention had fallen into a *semi-peaceful silence.*

Sophie was doodling in her notebook.
James was dramatically staring at the ceiling, mourning his lost ability to speak.
Caleb was casually tapping his fingers against the desk.
And Lily?

Lily was **freezing**.

The classroom's AC was **blasting**, and she *swore* the school did this *on purpose* to make detention more miserable.

She *tried* to tough it out. She *really* did.

But after five more minutes of **shivering**, Caleb suddenly sighed.

And then—

Without a word—

He **took off his hoodie** and dropped it onto Lily's desk.

Lily blinked. **Stared at it.** Then at Caleb.

"…What is this?" she asked.

Caleb raised an eyebrow. "A *spaceship*. What do you think?"

Lily huffed. "I'm *fine.*"

Caleb gave her a *look.* "Lily, you look like you're about to turn into an icicle."

Lily *crossed her arms.* "I don't need your-"

"Just put it on," Caleb said, **rolling his eyes**. "You literally admitted I saved your life once. What's one more time?"

Lily *groaned.* "I regret *everything.*"

But.

She put on the hoodie.

And.

It was **warm**.

It **smelled like him.** Like something faintly fresh and slightly minty.

Lily suddenly forgot how to exist.

James, watching this unfold, **immediately broke his silence**.

"BRO."

Sophie *gasped dramatically*. "CAUGHT IN 4K."

Caleb sighed. "I *knew* I should've made that Dare longer."

Lily **buried her face in the sleeves**, groaning. "Can this detention *please* end?"

Sophie and James?

**Absolutely thriving.**

Because *Operation: Set Them Up?*

Yeah. It was **going perfectly.**

# 9.The Truth beneath it all

**Four days.**

It had been four days since Caleb had last been at school.

And yet, somehow, it felt **longer.**

The first day was **confusing.**
The second day was **concerning.**
The third day was **wrong.**

And by the fourth day?

It felt like something had **snapped.**

It wasn't just that Caleb was gone—it was the way his absence felt **unnatural.**

Like something was **off.**

Like something **wasn't meant to be known.**

James wasn't talking much anymore. He had started the week brushing it off, making jokes, pretending like it wasn't a big deal. But now?

Lily could see it in the way his shoulders were tense, the way he kept **glancing at the hallways** as if hoping Caleb would **walk in at any moment.**

But he never did.

And then, just when the silence became unbearable—

Lily got the **note.**

And suddenly, everything made **even less sense.**


"Lily?"

She turned, startled.

Riya, a girl from her class, was standing there, holding a **folded piece of paper.**

Lily frowned. "What is it?"

Riya hesitated. "I found this under my desk this morning. It's weird. It has your name on it."

Lily's fingers felt **ice-cold** as she took it.

Her heart **pounded.**

She **unfolded it.**

And there, written in **familiar, messy handwriting**, were four words:

**"Find me if you can."**


**James Knew Something**

Lily didn't realize she was shaking until James snatched the note from her hands.

His expression changed **immediately.**

"…No way," he muttered.

Lily's voice barely came out. "It's his handwriting, right?"

James swallowed. "Yeah."

Sophie grabbed James's arm. "You know something, don't you?"

James hesitated.

Too long.

Lily's stomach twisted. "James."

A pause.

Then, finally—

"…I never told you," James said quietly, "but Caleb is rich."

Silence.

Lily blinked. "What?"

James let out a slow breath. "Yeah. His parents—" He hesitated, glancing at the note again before stuffing it into his pocket. "They're... *strict.*"

Sophie frowned. "Strict how?"

James' jaw tightened.

"They don't just want him to get good grades. They want him to be the **best**. In everything."

Lily's chest **tightened.**

"…Everything?"

James nodded. "Academics. Sports. Clubs. He has to be **first**—or it's not enough."

Lily felt like the floor was tilting.

She had always known Caleb was a **perfectionist**—but this? **This was something else.**

Sophie looked between them, her voice softer. "So… what? They moved him away to some fancy school?"

James shook his head. "No. If that were the case, he would've told me. I think…" His voice lowered. "I think something happened."

Lily **didn't like the sound of that.**

"Something like **what?**" she demanded.

James hesitated again.

Then, almost too quietly—

"…He washes his hands a lot."

Lily blinked. "What?"

James looked uncomfortable. "I didn't really think much about it before. But, like… he does it *all the time*. After a test. After practice. After literally anything that could go wrong. It got worse lately."

Lily stared at him. "How bad?"

James exhaled. "His hands were… dry. Really dry. Like—like he couldn't stop washing them. Like he was trying to—"

He stopped.

Lily swallowed hard. "Trying to what?"

James looked her in the eyes.

"Trying to wash something **away.**"


They ran to Caleb's house after school.

It was locked.

Lights off. No sign of life.

They asked the apartment manager.

**"The Millers? They moved out four days ago."**

Lily felt like the world was spinning.

James stared at the locked door, fists clenched.

Sophie whispered, "This doesn't make sense."

And Lily?

She looked down at the crumpled note in her pocket.

**"Find me if you can."**

And she knew—

**This wasn't over.**

The air outside Caleb's house felt **wrong**.

Lily stood still, staring at the **padlock on the front door**, her pulse **too loud** in her ears.

She could hear James breathing beside her—shaky, uneven. Sophie had her arms crossed, shifting uncomfortably like she didn't want to be here anymore.

But no one moved.

Because this **wasn't normal**.

This wasn't just a **missing friend** or a **transfer to another school**.

This was **something else**.

Something **none of them understood yet**.

And the worst part?

Caleb had left a **clue**—as if he wanted them to find him.

**"Find me if you can."**


James was the first to react.

He stepped forward, rattling the lock **too aggressively**, as if that would somehow undo it. "No. No way. *No way* they just *left*."

Lily turned to the apartment manager, struggling to keep her voice steady. "Do you know where they went?"

The woman barely looked up from her clipboard. "Didn't leave an address. Just packed up and left."

Lily's chest tightened. "They didn't say *why?*"

"Nope."

Lily wanted to push, wanted to demand more information—but then James let out a sharp, bitter laugh.

Of course. Of course **Caleb's parents** would do this.

They didn't care.

They never did.

James turned away, **kicking a rock so hard it hit a trash can across the street.** "I *knew* something was off. I *should've*—" He stopped, shaking his head.

Sophie hesitated. "James."

He ignored her. **Ran a hand through his hair. Took a deep breath.**

Then, finally, he looked at Lily. And when he spoke, his voice was **different—tired**.

"I need to tell you something else."


Lily had never seen James look **this serious** before.

It was unsettling.

James sat on the curb, elbows resting on his knees, staring at the ground like the words were **physically painful** to say.

"I didn't tell you everything before," he admitted.

Lily and Sophie sat down beside him, waiting.

James exhaled.

"Caleb's parents weren't just strict, okay? They were—" He paused, searching for the right word. "They were *relentless*."

Lily didn't speak.

James continued.

"They didn't care if he was tired. Didn't care if he didn't want to do something. He *had to*. Always. **First in every test. Every competition. Every single thing he touched.**"

Sophie's expression darkened. "That's insane."

James let out a bitter laugh. "Yeah, well. That's how it's been for *years*. But recently… it got worse."

Lily's throat felt dry. "How?"

James hesitated. Then—

"He started washing his hands."

Lily frowned. "What?"

James looked at her. "Constantly. Like… after every little thing. Like he was trying to get rid of something that **wasn't even there.**"

A strange **unease** crept into Lily's chest.

Sophie whispered, "Like a habit?"

James nodded. "A bad one. At first, I didn't think much of it. But then… I started noticing how dry his hands got. Like, really bad. Cracked skin. Red knuckles. He never talked about it, but I could tell—it wasn't just about **cleaning.**"

Lily stared at the locked house, something clicking in her mind.

Caleb had always been **calm. Controlled.** But maybe—just maybe—**it wasn't real.**

Maybe he had been breaking for a long time.

And none of them had seen it.


Lily pulled the note out of her pocket again, staring at the words.

**"Find me if you can."**

It wasn't just a message.

It was a **challenge.**

A clue.

Which meant—

Caleb wanted to be found.

James muttered under his breath, "Where would he go?"

Sophie frowned. "If his parents moved, wouldn't they take him?"

Lily's grip tightened on the note.

"…What if he ran away?"

Silence.

Then—

James stood up. "Then we find him."

Lily met his gaze.

And without another word, they knew—

**This wasn't over.**

Caleb was gone.

But he hadn't vanished.

He had **left a clue.**

And if he thought they were just going to sit back and accept his disappearance without a fight—

He was **wrong.**

Lily, James, and Sophie stood outside Caleb's locked house, the silence between them **heavy**.

They had one thing.

One single thing.

The note.

**"Find me if you can."**

It was so **Caleb,** so typical of him, that it made Lily's hands tighten into fists.

Sophie exhaled. "So, what now?"

James ran a hand through his hair, thinking. "We need to check somewhere. Somewhere he'd go if he was alone."

Lily frowned. "Somewhere his parents wouldn't look."

Sophie tilted her head. "Wouldn't he go to a relative's house?"

James shook his head. "Caleb doesn't have family here. It's just his parents. And they're… not the type to have close friends."

Lily looked down at the note again.

*Think, think, think.*

And then—

Her eyes widened.

She looked up at James. "What about the **old library?**"

James blinked. Then—

"Oh," he whispered. "Oh."


The old library was barely a **library** anymore.

It wasn't completely abandoned, but it might as well have been. It was tucked away at the edge of the city, **forgotten**, used only by students who needed complete silence.

And Caleb?

Caleb had **always** needed silence.

Lily, James, and Sophie arrived just before sunset. The sky was dimming, casting long shadows along the pavement.

Something about it felt... **wrong.**

Lily swallowed. "Are we sure about this?"

James didn't answer. He just **pushed open the door.**

The air inside was **cold**.

Dusty books. Dim lighting. Silence so thick it made their footsteps sound **too loud.**

Lily felt a chill crawl up her spine.

And then—

James grabbed her arm.

She turned—

And **froze.**

At the far end of the library, tucked between the shelves, was **Caleb's backpack.**

Just sitting there.

Waiting.

Lily's stomach twisted. "He was here."

James stepped forward, running his hand over the fabric. "Recently."

Sophie whispered, "Then where is he now?"

Lily turned in slow circles, scanning the room.

No sign of him.

No movement.

Just the backpack.

Just the **lingering presence of someone who shouldn't be gone.**

And then—

From behind them—

A book fell.

Loud. Sharp.

James **flinched**. Sophie **gasped.**

Lily turned so fast her heart nearly **jumped out of her chest.**

Nothing.

Just a book on the floor.

Just an empty aisle.

Just a silence that felt **too heavy.**

James whispered, "Caleb?"

No answer.

Lily's fingers curled around the note in her pocket.

Something wasn't right.

Something **wasn't right at all.**

Caleb had been here.

Recently.

His **backpack** sat against the dusty shelves like a forgotten **shadow**, like he had been here just minutes ago, like he had slipped between the aisles and **disappeared into thin air.**

Lily felt it in her bones—**he was close.**

And yet, he wasn't.


James took a slow step toward the book that had dropped.

The silence was **thick**, pressing against them, making the dimly lit library feel **too big, too empty.**

Lily **exhaled sharply.** "This doesn't make sense."

Sophie, standing close to her, crossed her arms. "You think he's hiding?"

James crouched down, picking up the book, dusting off the cover. He read the title aloud.

*"Perfection: The Price of Success."*

A chill ran down Lily's spine.

Her heartbeat picked up. **Too fast. Too loud.**

James looked up. His expression had changed. **Tight.**

Like he had just **realized something.**

"…I know where he is."


James turned to them, gripping the book tightly, his knuckles **white.**

"He's not hiding," James said, voice low. "He left the backpack on purpose."

Lily blinked. "What?"

James swallowed hard. "He knew we'd come looking. He's not *running* from us."

Lily's stomach **twisted.** "Then what is he doing?"

James looked at her.

And his next words sent a **chill through her bones.**

"He's waiting."


Lily's hands felt **cold** as she reached for the zipper of Caleb's backpack.

She didn't know what she was expecting—a phone, a note, a **reason** for all of this—

But when she pulled it open, she **froze.**

Inside was a small, folded paper.

She opened it.

Two words, scrawled in the same rushed, messy handwriting.

**"Music Room."**

James exhaled sharply. "Of course."

Lily turned to him, confused. "What do you mean *of course?*"

James hesitated. "There's something else I never told you."

Lily's stomach **dropped.** "James."

James clenched his jaw.

Then—**finally—he said it.**

 "Caleb… he doesn't just want to be first in academics. His parents—they push him in *everything*. Sports. Clubs. And…"

James swallowed.

"…Music."

Lily's mind raced. "Oh yeah, he mentioned it to me on that trip"

James nodded. "He plays the piano." He hesitated, then looked her directly in the eyes.

Lily's breath caught.

But then she thought about it. The way he tapped his fingers on the desk in the library like he was **keeping a beat.**

Sophie whispered, "So… his parents don't approve, do they?"

James let out a bitter laugh. "Approve? No. They *control* him. They don't care about what he wants. They only care about winning. Being the best. And singing? Music? To them, it's a *waste of time*."

Lily stared at the note again.

**"Music Room."**

He had been leaving clues.

**Not running.**

But **waiting to be found.**


They ran.

Through the empty school hallways, past darkened classrooms, their footsteps **echoing** through the silence.

Lily's heart pounded **too fast**, her mind racing with the **pieces finally fitting together.**

Caleb had been **pushed to the edge.**

And now?

He was **breaking free.**

James reached the music room first, shoving the door open—

And there he was.

Caleb.

Sitting at the old piano, fingers hovering over the keys.

His hands were **raw**, the skin dry and cracked—**just like James had said.**

And yet, he looked…

**Calm.**

Like for the first time in **forever**, he wasn't running.

Just **existing.**

His gaze lifted, meeting theirs.

No surprise.

No fear.

Just **acceptance.**

Lily took a slow step forward. "Caleb."

He didn't answer right away.

Then, after a long moment—

"I knew you'd find me."

His voice was hoarse. Tired.

But **not broken.**

Not anymore.



Lily stood still, waiting. Letting him have the time to **speak first.**

Caleb exhaled, pressing his fingers against his temples. "I had to get out."

James folded his arms. "And you thought *not telling us* was the best way to do that?"

Caleb gave a tired smile. "Would you have let me leave?"

James **shut up.**

Because the answer was **no.**

Lily finally spoke. "What happened?"

Caleb ran a hand through his hair. "My parents . The competitions. The pressure. It was getting worse." He paused, staring at his hands. "I—I was drowning. I didn't even realize how bad it had gotten until…" He hesitated.

Then, almost too quietly—

"Until I started washing my hands raw and still didn't feel clean."

Lily's chest **tightened.**

Caleb shook his head. "I couldn't do it anymore. So I left. I needed to just—**be.**"

Silence.

Then—

Sophie, softly: "What now?"

Caleb met Lily's gaze.

Lily glanced at sophie and looked at caleb. "No more hiding."

Caleb smiled.

Then, **very lightly**, he nudged Lily's arm. "And maybe… you'll be my first fan?"

Lily rolled her eyes. "Please. I was already your first fan."

Caleb blinked. Then—**grinned.**

And for the first time in **forever**, it reached his eyes.

And for the first time in **forever**, it reached his eyes.

For a moment, everything felt **lighter**.

The tension. The silence. The weight of Caleb's disappearance. It all **eased**, just a little, in the glow of that small, rare **real** smile on his face.

But Lily wasn't done.

She couldn't be.

Because there was still one question lingering **in the air**, heavy and unspoken.

She glanced at James and Sophie before finally looking at Caleb again.

Her voice was quiet. "Caleb… what about your parents?"

Just like that, the lightness **snapped.**

Caleb's fingers **stilled** on the piano keys.

He didn't look at her right away. Instead, his gaze dropped, focusing on his hands like he was counting the cracks on his skin.

Lily waited.

James **shifted uncomfortably.** Sophie bit her lip.

Then—finally—Caleb let out a slow, shaky exhale.

"They left."

Lily frowned. "What do you mean, *left?*"

Caleb gave a **hollow** smile. "Packed up. Moved out. Just like that." He lifted his hands, gesturing vaguely. "No warning. No goodbye. Just gone."

Lily's stomach **sank.**

"But… why?" she asked, voice barely above a whisper.

Caleb leaned back against the piano, sighing. "Because I wasn't *worth* staying for."

Silence.

James tensed. "That's **not true.**"

Caleb gave a **humorless laugh.** "To them? It is." He shook his head. "They had everything planned out for me. Top ranks. Medals. Scholarships. And I—" He gestured around them. "I ruined it."

Lily's chest tightened.

They had **left him**.

Just like that.

After everything they had forced on him, after every expectation they had crushed him under—

The second he **refused** to be what they wanted, they had **walked away.**

Sophie muttered, "That's so messed up."

Caleb just shrugged, like he had already accepted it. "Yeah, well. Guess I wasn't their 'perfect son' anymore."

Lily's fingers curled into fists. "You were *never* the problem, Caleb."

His eyes flickered up to hers.

She meant it. **He could tell.**

And maybe—just maybe—he was finally ready to believe it.

James let out a breath, rubbing the back of his neck. "Okay. So… what now? Where are you even staying?"

Caleb hesitated.

Lily's eyes widened. "Wait. **Are you staying here?**"

Caleb didn't answer.

Which meant—yes.

James groaned. "Dude."

Sophie put her hands on her hips. "You've been *living* in the music room?"

Caleb held up a hand. "Technically, I was **staying in the library** at first—"

"**Caleb!**" Lily smacked his arm.

He winced. "Okay, okay! Yeah, not my best idea."

James stared at him. "You could've just *told* us."

Caleb's smirk **faltered**. "I didn't think I could."

Lily crossed her arms. "And now?"

Caleb glanced at her. Then at James. Then Sophie.

And for the first time, he looked like he actually **saw them.** Like he realized they weren't just **people he left behind.**

They were here. **For him.**

Caleb exhaled, then gave a small, **genuine** nod.

"…Now, I think I can."

And just like that—

He wasn't alone anymore.

James let out a **long sigh**, rubbing the back of his neck like he was **already regretting what he was about to say.**

Then, he turned to Caleb.

"Alright, you idiot," James muttered. "You're staying with me."

Caleb blinked. "Wait, what?"

James crossed his arms. "You can't keep crashing in the **music room**. What's your plan? Sleep under the piano forever?"

Caleb hesitated. "…I mean, technically—"

James shot him a **look.**

"No. You're coming with me."

Caleb opened his mouth—probably to protest, because that's **what Caleb did**—but James **beat him to it.**

 "No arguments," James said firmly. "You need a place. I have space. End of discussion."

Caleb stared at him.

Lily did too.

Sophie whispered, "That was… weirdly responsible of you."

James rolled his eyes. "Shut up."

Caleb exhaled, running a hand through his hair. "James, I—I can't just—"

"You can," James said. "And you will."

Caleb **looked away,** jaw clenched, like he was **fighting with himself.**

Lily could see it—the hesitation, the stubbornness, the part of him that **wasn't used to accepting help.**

But James wasn't letting him **run this time.**

"Look," James said, **softer now**. "I know you think you have to do everything alone. But you don't. You have us."

Caleb's throat bobbed.

He didn't speak.

Didn't argue.

Just… **nodded.**

Lily let out a breath she hadn't realized she was holding.

And just like that—

Caleb **wasn't alone anymore.**

# 10. A new kind of normal

Caleb had a place to stay.

For the first time in **days**, he wasn't drifting, wasn't hiding, wasn't **alone.**

But that didn't mean everything was **fine.**

Because if there was one thing Caleb had learned, it was this—

Just because you **run**, doesn't mean your past won't **follow.**

Lily had expected things to feel **lighter** the next day.

Caleb had a real bed instead of a **school music room**. He had his friends around him. He had finally admitted **what he wanted.**

And yet—

Something still felt **off.**

She noticed it as soon as she walked into school.

James and Caleb were at their lockers, talking quietly.

Or rather—**James was talking.**

Caleb was **leaning against the lockers, eyes distant, like he wasn't really there.**

Lily hesitated, shifting on her feet before slowly walking up to them.

James glanced at her and sighed. "Great. You tell him."

Lily blinked. "Tell him what?"

James **gestured at Caleb.** "That he needs to stop looking like a ghost. I already told him, but he's being stubborn."

Caleb finally looked at her, **blinking sleepily.** "I don't look like a ghost."

Lily hesitated, glancing at him carefully. His face did look a little paler than usual, and his posture seemed **heavy**, like he wasn't fully awake yet.

Before she could stop herself, she **muttered softly**, "You, um… look a little tired."

Caleb's eyes flickered to hers, his lips parting slightly.

"Yeah?"

Lily's cheeks **felt warm.** She hesitated, lowering her gaze.

"…You should take care of yourself more."

Silence.

James and Sophie **exchanged a look.**

Then—

Caleb **rubbed the back of his neck, looking away.**

"…Thanks."

His voice was **quiet**. A little **awkward**. Almost… **shy.**

Lily's heart **skipped a beat.**

There was something about the way he said it—like he wasn't **used to being cared about.**

Her fingers tightened around the strap of her bag as she nodded, staring down at the floor.

James, of course, **noticed immediately. His grin was evil.**

"Oh my god."

Sophie **gasped dramatically.** "DID HE JUST—"

Lily **froze**.

Her ears **burned.** Her hands clutched the edges of her sleeves.

James smirked. "Two shy people in one conversation. This is *painful.*"

Sophie sighed dreamily. "It's *adorable.*"

Lily **looked down, too flustered to say anything.**

Caleb, still red, **mumbled into his hoodie.** "…Can we just *not* do this right now?"

James snorted. "Wow. Look at you. Blushing and everything."

Lily **turned even redder.**

She didn't say anything—just **nodded quickly** before walking away as fast as possible.

Caleb exhaled, tilting his head back against the lockers. "…I hate you both."

James **grinned.** "Nah, you love us."

Caleb mumbled something **too quiet to hear.**

But despite everything—

He was **smiling.**

And somewhere, just a little further down the hallway—

So was Lily.

Lily's ears were still warm.

She hadn't looked back after **practically escaping** from the conversation earlier, but she could still feel it. The teasing. The way James and Sophie were **definitely still smirking.**

And the way Caleb had looked at her.

Not mocking. Not smug.

Just… **soft.**

Her face **heated up again**, so she shook the thought away and focused on walking.

They were heading toward their classes when James suddenly **sighed dramatically.**

"Guys, I just realized something."

Sophie raised an eyebrow. "That you need a brain cell?"

James ignored her. "No. That in just **one more semester, we'll be seniors.**"

Lily blinked.

Oh.

Right.

The thought hit her like **a sudden gust of wind.**

This year… was almost over.


"Okay, but seriously," James continued, stuffing his hands into his pockets. "How did this year go by so fast?"

Sophie nodded. "Right? It feels like we just started, and now we're talking about *graduating* from 12th."

Lily **hadn't even thought about it before now.**

11th grade had always seemed like this **huge step,** something that would take forever to finish. But now?

Now, it was **already slipping through their fingers.**

"One more semester," Sophie mused, stretching her arms. "And after that?" She sighed dramatically. "*College.*"

Lily's chest **tightened.**

Caleb, who had been **quiet** for a while, finally spoke.

"…Feels weird."

James glanced at him. "What, graduating?"

Caleb nodded. "Yeah. Like, I still remember the first day. And now it's almost over."

Lily found herself **nodding too.**

She remembered it clearly. The start of 12h grade. The nerves. The **people she barely knew back then.**

And now?

Now, **they weren't just classmates anymore.**

Sophie sighed dramatically, linking her arms behind her head. "Honestly, the only special thing about 12th grade was **you two.**"

Lily **froze.** "Huh?"

Caleb blinked. "What?"

James smirked. "Oh, she's right. If we think about it, **nothing else** about 12th was even interesting. Except for you two."

Lily's breath **caught.**

She looked down at the floor, suddenly **very focused on her shoes.**

Caleb cleared his throat, suddenly **very interested in the wall.**

James and Sophie **grinned at each other.**

James nudged Sophie. "Man, if someone told me at the start of the year that *this* would be happening, I wouldn't have believed it."

Sophie snorted. "Same. But here we are."

Lily **stayed quiet, too flustered to say anything.**

Caleb, beside her, looked just as **shy.**

And even though neither of them spoke—

Their **faces** said everything.

The semester **crept up on them** faster than any of them had expected.

One day, they were laughing in the hallways, teasing each other about **graduation and the future.**

And the next?

They were **buried under textbooks, lost in notebooks, drowning in practice tests.**

Because **this** wasn't just any semester.

This was **the semester.**

The one that decided **everything.**

Three days.

**Three days of absolute chaos.**

The final semester before **graduating to the real world** had arrived, and with it—

**Exams.**

Not just **one**.

Not even **two.**

But **every** subject thrown at them **back-to-back**, with barely enough time to **breathe in between.**

It was exhausting. It was stressful. It was **exactly what they had been dreading.**

And yet—somehow, they made it through.

**Day 1: The War Begins (Mathematics & English)**

The **worst possible** combination.

Math in the morning. English in the afternoon.

Two completely different types of **mental suffering.**

She stared at her Math paper, the numbers **blurring together.**

She knew this. She had studied this.

But why did everything look **so different** now?

She took a deep breath, gripping her pen.

*One question at a time, Lily. You can do this.*

By the time the English paper came, her brain was **fried.**

When she flipped to the **essay section**, she nearly groaned.

*Write about the most memorable day of your life.*

Her first thought?

**The day Caleb disappeared.**

Her second thought?

Her **face burned.**

No. No, absolutely not.

She quickly picked **another topic.**


Math was **fine.**

Mostly.

He knew all the answers, but he had **checked them too many times**, his anxiety whispering that something was **wrong, wrong, wrong.**

By the time he turned in the paper, his hands felt **cold.**

English was **worse.**

Not because it was difficult—**but because it was English.**

And English meant **writing.**

And writing meant **thinking.**

His essay?

He didn't even want to look at it.

Because when the prompt said *write about something that changed your life—*

His mind went straight to **her.**

## Day 2: The Nightmare (Physics & Chemistry)

If Math and English were **bad**, then Physics and Chemistry were **hell.**

James **stared** at his Physics paper.

Then at the ceiling.

Then back at the paper.

"...I have made a mistake."

He scribbled down an answer, hoping for the best.

By the time the Chemistry exam started, his soul had **already left his body.**

Sophie was **thriving.**

She **loved** Chemistry.

Unlike the others, she was actually **relaxed**, flipping through her answers **twice for fun.**

By the time she walked out of the exam hall, she felt **perfectly fine.**

Then she saw the others.

James looked like he had fought in a **war.**

Lily looked like she was **still fighting it.**

Caleb just looked **done.**

"...You all look terrible."

James groaned. "Thank you, Sophie. Very helpful."


**Day 3: The Final Blow (Biology & History)**

The last day.

**Biology in the morning.
History in the afternoon.**

Two subjects. Two completely **different types of stress.**

**Lily's POV:**

She **actually liked Biology.**

But the diagrams? **The labeling?**

Her hands were **shaking** by the time she finished.

And then—

**History.**

History was **long.**

By the end of the three-hour exam, she had **written so much** that she was **convinced her hand would fall off.**


Caleb **excelled** at History.

It was **facts. Dates. Logic.**

But Biology?

…Let's just say he was **glad it was over.**

By the time they walked out of the exam hall, **the weight finally lifted.**


**The Aftermath**

Three days.

Countless exams.

Too many sleepless nights.

And now?

It was **done.**

Lily sat outside with the others, the cold breeze **finally feeling nice** instead of stressful.

James flopped onto the bench dramatically. "We survived."

Sophie smirked. "Some of us better than others."

James groaned. "I will never forgive Physics."

Caleb leaned back, stretching his arms. "It's over."

Lily smiled, **tugging her sleeves over her hands.**

It really was.

11th grade was almost over. **One semester left.**

And for the first time—

She wasn't **scared** of what came next.

The **exams were over.**

And just like that, the school **felt different.**

No one was rushing to cram formulas at the last minute. No one was whispering answers under their breath before an exam started.

It was **quiet.**

But it wasn't the **tense kind of quiet** that came before an exam.

It was the **relieved kind.**

Like the whole school had **finally exhaled.**

Lily **liked it.**

The four of them sat on the school's front steps, letting the **cool breeze** wash over them.

James, as expected, had **flopped onto his back**, groaning dramatically. "I think my brain melted somewhere in the middle of that History paper."

Sophie **rolled her eyes.** "You always say that, and yet, you somehow never fail."

James **grinned.** "What can I say? I'm a natural genius."

Caleb let out a **tired chuckle**, shaking his head. "Or you're just lucky."

James **shrugged.** "Same thing."

Lily **hugged her knees to her chest,** listening quietly as they talked.

Everything felt… **lighter.**

The exams were done. The semester was almost over.

And for once, they could **breathe.**


Sophie stretched, tilting her head up toward the sky. "You know what's weird?"

James raised an eyebrow. "Your taste in music?"

Sophie ignored him. "This is our **last** semester of 12th."

Lily blinked.

Oh.

Right.

They had been **so focused on exams** that she hadn't really thought about it.

Just **one more semester.**

And then—

COLLEGE

Their **last year of school.**

Caleb sighed, running a hand through his hair. "It doesn't feel real."

James hummed in agreement. "Yeah. Feels like we *just* got here."

Lily found herself nodding. "Everything went by so fast."

Sophie smirked. "Well, *most* of it was boring. Except for you two."

Lily **froze.**

Caleb, beside her, **stiffened.**

James **grinned.** "Oh, she's right. 12th grade was **pretty basic.** Except for *you two.*"

Lily **lowered her head,** suddenly very **interested in her sleeves.**

Caleb coughed, looking away, **his ears turning red.**

James and Sophie **exchanged a knowing look.**

"Ah," James said. "There it is."

Sophie grinned. "They're being shy again."

Lily **squeezed her hands together**, her face burning.

Caleb muttered something under his breath.

James **leaned in.** "What was that?"

"…Nothing," Caleb mumbled.

James snickered. "Uh-huh. Sure."

Sophie sighed, stretching her arms. "Anyway, now that we're *officially free*—we should celebrate."

James **perked up.** "You mean, like, a party?"

Sophie shook her head. "No, no. Just something small. The four of us."

She turned to Lily and Caleb. "What do you guys think?"

Lily **fidgeted**, still trying to calm down from the teasing. "Um… sounds nice."

Caleb nodded. "Yeah. Let's do it."

Sophie clapped her hands. "Perfect."

James smirked. "See? **Look at us.** Being responsible seniors already."

Caleb snorted. "We're *not* seniors yet."

James shrugged. "Close enough."

Lily **smiled softly.**

Everything would **change again now.**

But for now?

She was **okay with this.**

The bell rang, signaling the **end of the day**, but for once, no one **rushed** to leave.

There was no urgency, no 'what did you get for this question?', no panicked whispers about **exams.**

Just the sound of footsteps, distant chatter, and the occasional **laugh** echoing through the halls.

Lily and the others walked **slowly**, taking their time, letting the reality of it all **sink in.**

Then, they'd be **real adults.**

Then, they'd be on their **last day of school.**

It felt… **strange.**

Like something that should have happened **so much later,** yet was suddenly **right in front of them.**

James stretched his arms behind his head as they walked down the hallway. "So. What now?"

Sophie shrugged. "Well, graduation , the last trip and college"

Caleb **let out a tired chuckle.** "That's optimistic."

Lily, walking beside them, **nodded quietly.**

She wasn't exactly sure **what came next either.**

Everything had moved **so fast.**

Just a few months ago, she barely spoke to Caleb. **Barely knew him.**

Now, she couldn't **imagine school without him.**

The thought made her **fidget slightly**, her hands tightening around the strap of her bag.

Sophie smirked, glancing between Caleb and Lily. "You two are awfully quiet."

Caleb **tensed.** "Huh?"

Lily's **face warmed.** "I—I was just thinking."

Sophie **raised an eyebrow.** "Thinking about what?"

Lily hesitated.

James **grinned.** "Lemme guess. Caleb?"

Lily **froze.**

Caleb, beside her, **stiffened immediately.**

"…What?" he said, voice slightly higher than usual.

James and Sophie exchanged a **knowing look.**

Lily, **too flustered to argue,** simply **lowered her gaze, her ears burning.**

Caleb, still **shocked**, looked away, rubbing the back of his neck. "You guys are—" He sighed. "Never mind."

James **snickered.** "Adorable."

Sophie sighed dramatically. "I know, right?"

Lily said **nothing.**

Caleb, at this point, also seemed to accept that **arguing was pointless.**

So they simply **walked in silence, side by side—** flustered, embarrassed, but somehow…

**Not minding it as much as before.**


As they stepped outside, the cool **evening breeze** brushed past them, carrying the soft hum of students chatting, the **faint sound of the basketball team practicing**, and the occasional **ringing of a bicycle bell.**

Sophie exhaled. "College"

Lily tucked a strand of hair behind her ear. **College.**

James grinned. "We should do something after it happens. Something fun."

Caleb raised an eyebrow. "Like what?"

Sophie smirked. "Oh, I'll think of something."

James **snapped his fingers.** "Ooooh, what about a road trip?"

Lily blinked. "A… road trip?"

James nodded. "Yeah! One last adventure before we become proper adults."

Caleb **gave him a look.** "You? Serious?"

James gasped, putting a hand over his heart. "That was *unnecessarily* rude."

Lily giggled softly, and Caleb, hearing it, **glanced at her for a moment**—before quickly looking away.

Sophie **rolled her eyes.** "We'll plan something. But for now, let's just enjoy the fact that we *survived* the semester."

James stretched. "I'll take that."

Caleb nodded. "Same."

Lily, **watching them laugh and joke like they always did**, realized something.

This year had been **nothing like she expected.**

And yet—

It had been **everything she didn't know she needed.**

As they walked off together, heading home, she let herself smile.

Because **whatever came next—**

She was **ready.**

# 11."Where it all started"

The sky was **bright**, the air filled with a soft **buzz of excitement.**

Students dressed in **black-gold graduation gowns** roamed the school grounds, some **laughing**, some **wiping away tears**, others taking **endless pictures**, trying to freeze the moment before it passed.

Graduation day.

The day they had spent **years working toward.**

And yet—

Caleb stood in the middle of it all, feeling like he was in a **dream.**


Somewhere in the background, James was talking to someone. Sophie was adjusting her gown, **probably criticizing the fabric.**

Caleb barely listened.

He should've felt **something big.**

Happiness. Excitement. Relief.

But all he felt was—**off.**

Like something wasn't **real.**

Like he had spent so long **fighting, running, surviving**, that now that it was all **over**—

He didn't know **what to do with himself.**

"Dude," James suddenly nudged him. "We did it."

Caleb blinked, snapping out of his thoughts. "Huh?"

James rolled his eyes. "I said—we *did it.*"

Sophie smirked. "Pretty well, too. I checked our scores this morning. We all did **way better than expected.**"

Caleb let that sink in.

The exams. The late nights. The stress.

They had made it through.

**They had actually done well.**

And for the first time, Caleb felt it—

The realization.

It was over.


The speaker crackled, cutting through the noise.

Then, a familiar voice—

**Miguel's.**

*"All 12th graders, please assemble in the auditorium for the graduation ceremony."*

James let out a deep sigh, shaking his head. "Man, hearing his voice on the speaker again feels *weird*."

Then, he nudged Caleb with his elbow.

*"Where it all started."*

Caleb stiffened slightly.

Because James was **right.**

The first time he had ever heard **Miguel's voice over the speaker**, he was in the start of 12th grade, standing **right here.**

And back then, **everything was different.**

He glanced around, suddenly feeling **out of place.**

Lily wasn't here.

Just James beside him, his usual confident smirk in place.

Then—

Sophie now realizing

"Wait, wait—**did you see Lily?**"

Sophie.

"No," James said immediately. "Where is she?"

Sophie **shook her head.** "I don't know—"

Caleb felt something **shift inside him.**

Lily wasn't the type to **just disappear**.

Before he could even process it, a **firm hand** landed on his shoulder.

"Miller, move," came Mr. Carter's voice. "You too, James, Sophie—get to the auditorium. Now."

Caleb **hesitated.** "But—"

"Go."

And just like that, **he was being pushed forward.**

The auditorium was packed.

Students filled the seats, teachers stood near the stage, and the principal stood at the podium, delivering a speech that **Caleb wasn't hearing at all.**

His mind was **somewhere else.**

Lily wasn't here.

She should've been **here.**

Where was she?

He scanned the room, eyes moving **through the crowd,** searching for something—anything.

Nothing.

A strange feeling settled in his chest.

Then—

Movement at the entrance.

A flash of **dark hair. A black gown.**

Someone **running.**

And just like that—

Everything **zoned out.**


Caleb's world **blurred.**

The crowd, the voices, the speech—**all faded.**

Because there she was.

Lily.

Holding her **graduation cap**, her gown swaying behind her as she ran into the auditorium, her breath slightly ragged from **probably sprinting across campus.**

But all Caleb could see was—

**Her.**

His heartbeat **stuttered.**

Because for a moment, he wasn't here.

He was back at the **sports competition.**

The first time he had ever seen her.

The way **she smiled.**

And now—

It was the **same.**

She was looking at him now, as he raised his hand, signalling that they all were here

**right at him.**

And then—

She **smiled.**

That same, soft, **unintentional** smile.

The exact same one from the **sports competition.**

Something inside Caleb **stirred.**

And for the first time in the entire day—

Everything **felt real.**

Caleb **hadn't blinked** since he saw her.

Lily **slowed down**, breath still a little uneven from running, but the moment she reached them, she **smiled.**

"Sorry, guys," she said, tucking a strand of hair behind her ear.

Sophie threw her arms up. "Lily! Where were you? *Why today* of all days?"

Lily let out a **small laugh.** "My cycle got punctured."

James groaned. "Classic. Only you."

Lily just **smiled**, first at James—then at Caleb.

And **for some reason**, Caleb felt like his **chest tightened just a little.**

He didn't even realize he was still **staring at her** until she turned back to Sophie, standing beside her, fixing her gown like nothing had happened.

And then—

The principal's voice **boomed** through the microphone.


*"Seniors."*

Caleb **exhaled.**

*"You may now remove your hats."*

For a second—just a second—there was **silence.**

And then—

The sky turned **black with hats.**

**Millions of them.**

Millions of people **cheering, screaming, laughing.**

A sea of movement. A **moment too big to process.**

But somehow, in all of that—

Caleb found **her.**

Lily was **already looking at him.**

And as their hands **threw their hats into the air**, she **mouthed something.**

**"It's all over."**

Then, she **smiled.**

Not just any smile.

That **pretty, soft, heart-achingly familiar smile.**

The kind that made **everything stop.**

And before Caleb even realized it—

He was smiling too.

As their hats **fell back down, as they caught them, as the world spun and screamed and celebrated around them—**

It all felt so **unbelievable.**

Because somehow, in the mess of it all—

**They had made it.**

James suddenly **threw an arm over Caleb's shoulder.** "Dude. We actually did it."

Caleb blinked, shaken out of whatever **spell he had been under.**

James was **grinning**, eyes slightly wide like he couldn't believe it either.

Sophie grabbed Lily's hand, **swinging it lightly.** "Lily, can you believe it? "

Lily let out a **small laugh,** shaking her head. "It… doesn't feel real."

James sighed dramatically. "Ugh, don't get sentimental on me."

Sophie smirked. "Oh, please.."

James gasped. "How *dare* you?"

Lily giggled softly, and Caleb—**he didn't even realize he was staring again.**

Because for some reason, the way she laughed in **this moment—**

With her hair slightly messy from running, the sunset casting a **soft glow** over her face, her gown slightly oversized on her frame—

It all looked so…

**Perfect.**

And suddenly, it hit him.

This year.

Everything that had happened.

The late-night studying. The teasing. The mornings where they **waited outside the school gates together**. The moments where they **locked eyes across a classroom** and quickly looked away.

The way his chest **always felt light** when she was near.

It all came rushing back.

And he finally **realized something.**

Something he **should've understood** a long time ago.

Lily wasn't just someone he **cared about.**

She was someone he **wanted to stay close to.**

Even after this year. Even after **everything changed again.**

She was the person who made all of this **feel real.**


As the ceremony ended, students **slowly drifted away,** leaving the school grounds in groups, still **buzzing with excitement.**

James stretched, yawning. "I vote we go get food. I'm starving."

Sophie raised an eyebrow. "You're *always* starving."

James **ignored her.**

Lily and Caleb walked slightly behind them, **not speaking much.**

Not out of awkwardness—

But out of that **unspoken understanding** that sometimes, words weren't needed.

Lily glanced at Caleb.

He looked… **different.**

Not bad different.

Just—like something had **finally settled in him.**

Like he had finally **let go of something.**

She bit her lip, then, almost too softly—

"…You okay?"

Caleb turned to her, **startled**.

For a moment, he didn't answer.

Then, slowly, he exhaled.

"…Yeah."

And for the first time in a long time—

He actually meant it.

138

# 12. What comes next

Graduation was over.

The celebrations, the laughter, the **feeling of disbelief—** all of it had finally settled.

And now?

Now, **reality was here.**

Because **college applications had begun.**

And for the first time, they weren't just thinking about **high school ending.**

They were thinking about **what came after.**


Lily sat cross-legged on her bed, sketchbook open beside her, a telephone pressed against her ear.

"Are we all on the call?" Sophie's voice rang through the speaker.

"Yep," James replied, **mouth full of something.** Caleb giggling looking at him "Wait, hold on, I need to swallow this."

Caleb sighed. "Do they even want to know what you're eating?"

**"No."**

Sophie groaned. "This is why we don't take you seriously."

Lily **smiled softly,** listening as James finished his food before finally speaking.

"So," James said. "Colleges. We're actually doing this."

For a second, there was **silence.**

Because yeah—

They were actually doing this.

"I already applied," Sophie said, her voice confident. "There's this insane sports college two states away—great programs, even a few Olympians came from there."

James whistled. "Damn, aiming high."

"Obviously."

Lily smiled. "This is what you are supposed to do."

"Right?" Sophie said. "I can't imagine myself doing anything else."

She **sounded sure.**

And Lily… **admired that.**

Because while she loved art, the idea of actually **pursuing it in college?**

It was… terrifying.

But before she could overthink, James spoke.

"So, I kind of had a *moment* recently," James started.

Sophie sighed. "That's never a good thing."

James ignored her. "I found out about this **company.**"

"What company?" Caleb asked.

"It's called **Microsoft.**"

Silence.

Then—

"…Never heard of it," Sophie admitted.

James huffed. "Yeah, well, it's new. But they're working on **AI.**"

Lily tilted her head. "Like… robots?"

 "Not exactly." James sat up, excitement creeping into his voice. "It's about **making computers smarter, making them think.** I don't know—it's just *cool.* I wanna be part of something like that."

There was a pause.

Then, Caleb said, **genuinely impressed,** "That's actually really interesting."

James grinned. "I know, right?"

Sophie snorted. "Wow. First time I've seen you talk about school like you actually care."

James gasped. "How *dare* you?"

Lily giggled.

Then—

Caleb took the telephone from james.


"My parents don't care anymore,don't even know where I am" Caleb said suddenly.

Everyone **froze.**

Lily felt her chest tighten. "Caleb…"

He let out a breath, his voice **lighter** than they expected.

"No, I mean… it's a good thing. For once, I actually get to do what I want."

James hesitated. "And that is?"

A pause.

Then—

Caleb smiled, even though no one could see it.

"I applied to a musical college."

"Oh yeah, he did!" James responded too

Sophie gasped. "You **actually** did it?"

Caleb chuckled. "Yeah. I mean… if I don't try now, when will I?"

Lily felt something warm in her chest.

She had **always** known this was his dream.

And now?

He was **chasing it.**

Sophie cheered. "Okay, we *have* to celebrate this later."

James laughed. "Agreed."

Then, finally, **Lily's turn came.**


"…I applied to an art school."

Silence.

Not the bad kind.

The **surprised-but-proud** kind.

Sophie **grinned.** "You did?"

Lily hesitated, fingers tightening around her sketchbook. "Yeah. I… don't know if I'll get in, but—"

"You *will*," Caleb said, voice certain.

Lily's breath hitched. "You think so?"

"I know so."

And he said it in a way that made **her believe it too.**

Sophie clapped her hands. "Okay, I'm *officially* excited now."

James sighed dramatically. "Wow. We're all actually *going places*."

Caleb smirked. "Even you."

James **snorted.** "I know, *shocking*."

Lily smiled, listening to them talk, feeling **something settle in her heart.**

They were growing up.

Going separate ways.

And yet—

Right now, in this moment, everything still felt **the same.**

Like they would always be **connected.**

Even if the future was uncertain—

They were stepping into it **together.**

# 13.Different roads, same us

College had begun.

New schedules. New people. New expectations.

For the first time in years, they weren't walking the same hallways, waiting at the same bus stops, or spending their lunch breaks together.

And even though they all **knew** this day was coming—

It still felt **strange.**


Lily had imagined **art school** to be a dream.

And in many ways, it was.

Everywhere she turned, there were **colors, ideas, creativity in motion.** It was inspiring, overwhelming, and… honestly, **kind of terrifying.**

Everyone here was **good.**

Like, really good.

And even though she loved art, the pressure to **prove herself** was **always there.**

Still—when she finally picked up her pencils and started sketching, she remembered **why she was here.**

This was her **passion.**

And she wouldn't let **self-doubt** take that away from her.

She just wished she had time to actually **breathe.**

Or, you know—see her friends.

But every time she thought of suggesting a meet-up, someone was **already busy.**


Music school was **nothing like he expected.** He thought calling the supposedly college, "school" was weird

He had imagined something laid-back, something that finally let him **breathe.**

Instead, it was a **storm.**

Talent everywhere. Auditions for performances every other day. The expectation to **stand out.**

For the first time in a long time, he wasn't expected to be **perfect in school subjects.**

But here?

Here, he had to be **perfect at what he loved.**

It was thrilling.

It was terrifying.

And it was **exhausting.**

At night, he sometimes caught himself **reaching for his phone, wanting to text Lily, James, or Sophie.**

But every time he checked the chat, someone was already saying **"I can't this weekend. Maybe next time?"**

And so—he just put the phone back down.

Maybe next time.


James **liked** his AI course in his college.

It was **fascinating,** filled with people who thought **just like him.**

But it was **also a lot.**

Late-night coding. Intense research. Professors who expected you to **think ten steps ahead**

Most nights, his room was **lit only by his laptop screen**, eyes glued to thousands of lines of code, trying to make sense of something that **hadn't even existed five years ago.**

It was **exciting.**

It was **insane.**

It was **too much to even think about planning a trip.**

Not that they didn't try.

They did.

It just… never worked.

Sports college was **no joke.**

She woke up early. She trained for hours. She barely had time to eat, let alone go on a trip.

She wanted to.

God, she wanted to.

But every time the group chat came alive with, **"Okay, THIS weekend?"**

She had to type, **"Sorry, can't. Tournament."**

And then someone else would say, **"I have exams."**

And then—

**Nothing.**

They planned it **so many times.**

The messages were always the same:

**"Next week?"**
**"No, I have exams."**
**"What about the week after?"**

"I have practice."
"The week after that?"
"Sorry, I have rehearsals."

Until, slowly—

The messages just **stopped coming.**

Not because they **forgot.**

But because they all **knew the answer before they even asked.**

They had all grown up.

All moved forward.

And even though they still talked, still laughed over voice calls and texts—

That trip?

It was never going to happen.

Maybe in the future.

Maybe not.

But somehow—

That was **okay.**

The trip was canceled.

And with it—everything else.

At first, it was **just a few days** of silence.

Then, a week.

Then, a month.

Until one day—

Lily unlocked her phone, scrolled through her messages, and realized—

No one had sent anything in **weeks.**

No "how are you?"
No "I saw something that reminded me of you."
No "let's plan again."

Just… **nothing.**

And that was that.


Caleb stopped checking his phone late at night.

James stopped trying to start conversations.

Sophie stopped expecting replies.

Lily stopped opening the chat entirely.

There was no fight. No dramatic goodbye.

Just life—**pulling them apart.**

And maybe, that was always **meant to happen.**

Maybe some people were only **meant to stay in your life for a while.**

And then?

Then they became **just a memory.**


Time passed.

Days turned into weeks. Weeks into months.

And just like that—

High school became **a thing of the past.**

No more familiar hallways. No more shared lunch tables. No more waiting at the school gates, no more whispered conversations during lectures, no more **them.**

Lily, Caleb, James, and Sophie had once been **inseparable.**

Now, they were just **people who used to know each other.**

And somehow—

That was **okay.**

Lily sat at her dorm room desk, pencil scratching against paper.

Her sketchbook was **full of memories she never said out loud.**

A messy doodle of a **blue graduation cap.**
A half-drawn piano.
A small, scribbled "12th grade" in the corner of one page.

She never showed anyone these.

Because they weren't **important anymore.**

At least, that's what she told herself.


Caleb's fingers moved over the piano keys.

The music **filled the empty practice room**, soft, familiar.

But then, halfway through a melody—

He stopped.

He didn't know why.

Just that something **felt different.**

Like a song he used to know by heart, but couldn't quite remember anymore.

And maybe—

Maybe that was just how things were now.

James' phone buzzed.

Not from **them.**

It hadn't, in a long time.

At some point, the group chat had **fallen silent.**

No one had **left it.**

No one had deleted it.

It just… stopped.

He stared at it for a moment.

Then, without thinking, he sent a message.

**"Hope you're all doing okay."**

A minute passed. Then two. Then five.

No reply.

James sighed, locking his phone.

It was fine.

He was fine.

Sophie knew what had happened.

She just didn't talk about it.

One day, they were planning trips and calling each other nonstop.

And the next?

They weren't.

No fight. No drama.

Just life.

She scrolled through their old messages once—just once.

Then, she put her phone away.

Because that part of her life was **over.**

And that was that.

It is no longer okay but what is there to do



That was that.

# 14.Everything Changes

Three months.

Three months since graduation.
Three months since their last real conversation.
Three months since everything **changed.**

Lily should've been **happy.**

She was in **art school.**

The place she had always **dreamed of being.**

And she was good—**really good.**

Her professor had even **praised** her last drawing, saying it
had an "eye for emotion."

But no matter how much she tried to **focus on her career**,
there was always this **lingering feeling.**

Like something had been **left behind.**

Like something **was missing.**

Lily stared at her phone screen, **thumb hovering over the
messages.**

The group chat was still there.

The last message?

A simple "**Good luck with everything!**" from Sophie.

That was **months ago.**

Lily kept telling herself to **move on.**

To focus on **her work, her future, herself.**

But some nights, she still found herself **checking her notifications**, hoping for something **that was never coming back.**

And the worst part?

She didn't even know **if she wanted to let go.**


Caleb sat at the grand piano, fingers **dancing over the keys**, playing a melody that **wasn't written down anywhere.**

It was just **his.**

Music school had been **relentless**, but rewarding.

For the first time in his life, **he was being praised for something he actually cared about.**

"You have talent, Caleb," his piano master had told him. "Not just in playing, but in your voice too."

Caleb had **brushed it off at first.**

Singing was **his dream**, sure—

But no one ever **took dreams seriously.**

Until his piano master said something that **changed everything.**

"I know a director. He's casting for a musical film."

Caleb had **stopped playing immediately.**

His master had smiled, placing a hand on his shoulder.

"I think you should audition."

For days, Caleb **hesitated.**

This wasn't **some small opportunity.**

This was **huge.**

But was he ready?

Was he good enough?

Or was he just **setting himself up for disappointment?**

He had spent **so long being told what to do.**

Now, when he finally had a **choice—**

It terrified him.

It took **three sleepless nights** and **a hundred self-doubts.**

But in the end, Caleb finally **texted his master back.**

**"I'll do it."**

And just like that—

His life was about to **change forever.**

And Lily's? Hah

# 15.One year later

A year had passed.

One whole year since graduation.
One whole year since their last real conversation.
One whole year since everything **fell apart.**

Caleb had **moved on.**

Lily?

She wasn't sure if she had.



Lily sat in the art studio, charcoal dust on her fingers, her latest sketch half-finished.

It was a portrait.

Unintended, but **familiar.**

Sharp jawline.
Tired eyes.
Fingers hovering over invisible piano keys.

She sighed, gripping her eraser and **smudging the details away.**

She hadn't meant to draw **him.**

She never meant to.

But sometimes, when she let her mind wander—

It always found its way **back to the past.**

Art school was **fine.**

She had the talent, the skill, the technique.

But… no friends.

Not because she didn't want them.

Just because she had **forgotten how to make them.**

She wasn't the girl from high school anymore.

No Sophie. No James.

No Caleb.

Just **herself.**

Alone.

And somehow—

She was **used to it now.**


**"Lights! Cameras! Action!"**

The set burst into life.

Caleb **exhaled**, gripping the microphone tightly as the music swelled around him.

Scene **324.**

Take **seven.**

The past year had been **everything he once dreamed of.**

Singing. Acting? **His name in the credits.**

**Finally being seen.**

Finally getting what he **deserved.**

And yet—

As the director called "Cut!" and his co-stars laughed, clapping each other on the back—

Caleb stood there, feeling **nothing.**

He had **moved out** of James's place months ago.

Didn't even tell him in person.

Just packed up and left.

No calls.
No texts.
Nothing.

After everything James had done for him, he had **walked away.**

Just like his parents.

Just like Sophie.

Just like…

Caleb shook his head.

*No.*

This was how it was supposed to be.

This was the life he **worked for.**

So why did it feel like he had **lost something in the process?**

# 16.Still Life

Lily had learned to **exist in silence.**

She wasn't invisible, not really. People **knew** her. They admired her work, they complimented her in passing, but it was **never personal.**

Never **real.**

She had **no friends here.**

At first, she thought she just needed time.

That maybe, eventually, she'd meet someone who **understood her.**

But a year had passed.

And still—nothing.

No group chats filled with late-night conversations.
No random calls just to check in.
No one to ask her, **"Are you okay?"**

Just her.

And her art.

And the **empty spaces where people used to be.**


She hadn't intended for it to **look like him.**

But when she stepped back and really saw it—

The sharp angles. The distant gaze. The tension in the hands.

It was Caleb.

**Of course, it was.**

Lily **stared at it for too long,** fingers tightening around her brush.

She should cover it up. **Blur the features.** Change it into something—**someone—else.**

But she didn't.

She just **let it be.**

Because, deep down, she already knew—

Some things refuse to be erased.


The painting ended up in the **art showcase.**

Lily hadn't planned on submitting it.

But her professor saw it, stopped in front of it for **longer than usual**, and simply said—

*"This one."*

She didn't argue.

Didn't even ask **why.**

And so, when the night of the exhibition arrived, her painting stood **among the others**, framed in soft lighting, a quiet reminder of something she had **lost.**

She wasn't even sure why she came to see it.

Maybe to make sure it was still **hers.**

Maybe to convince herself **it didn't mean anything.**

But then—

A voice.

Not behind her.

But beside her.

**"This is yours, isn't it?"**

Lily turned.

And found herself **face-to-face with a stranger?**

The stranger stood beside her, hands tucked into his pockets, eyes fixed on the painting.

Lily **blinked**, thrown off for a second.

She had expected polite compliments from professors. Maybe an art student asking about her brushwork.

But this?

This was… different.

**He wasn't just looking at the painting.**

He was **studying it.**

Like he was trying to **understand something deeper.**

Lily hesitated, fingers fidgeting with the hem of her sleeve.

"…Yeah. It's mine."

The stranger let out a small hum, tilting his head slightly.

"It's intense." He paused. "Not just the strokes—the whole mood. Feels like… something unresolved."

Lily swallowed.

He wasn't wrong.

She had painted it in **one of those nights**—the ones where she kept checking her phone, where she felt like there was something she was **supposed to say to someone, but never did.**

She had poured **everything into it.**

And now, a complete stranger was standing here, **seeing it.**

Lily exhaled. "It's, um… kind of personal."

The guy gave a small smile. "The best ones always are."

She blinked.

Something about his presence was oddly **calm.**

Unlike the buzzing crowd around them, he wasn't here to just **glance and move on.**

He was **actually here.**

And for the first time in **months**, Lily felt like someone was really **seeing her.**

Not just her art.

**Her.**

As he turned towards the other pieces, lily couldn't help but notice something on his neck. A tatoo?

A bouquet of a flower?

"Are those…lilies?"

Caleb's phone buzzed.

He ignored it.

Scene **324** had drained him. He had barely slept, barely eaten, just gone from one set to another, repeating lines, hitting notes, playing the part.

It should've felt like **success.**

Instead, it felt like… nothing.

His manager's voice crackled through his earpiece.

*"Caleb, the press event is tomorrow. Get some rest."*

Caleb hummed an empty **"Yeah."**

He took out his earpiece and leaned against the window of the van.

The city lights blurred past.

And for some reason, he thought about a **painting.**

Not one he had seen.

But one he **could imagine.**

Distant. Faded. Unfinished.

Just like the person who made it.

And before he could stop himself, his fingers hovered over his phone screen.

Over a name he hadn't touched in a **year.**

**Lily.**

He stared at it for too long.

Then—

He put the phone down.

And let the moment **pass.**


The conversation with the stranger **stayed with her.**

Not because of what he said—**but because of what he saw.**

Something unresolved.

Something unfinished.

She had thought the past was just that—**the past.**

But standing in front of her own painting, having a stranger see right through her, she realized—

**She had never really moved on.**

Not from the people she lost.

Not from the silence that replaced them.

Not from him.

Not from **Caleb.**

She exhaled, pressing her fingers against her temples.

*No. This is ridiculous.*

She had work to do.

Her next assignment. Her next sketch.

Her **future.**

She needed to stop waiting for something that **wasn't coming back.**

So, for the first time in months, she did something she **never thought she'd do.**

She opened the group chat.

And deleted it.

That was that.


Caleb scrolled through the messages.

**Not his.**

Other people's.

His manager. The director. PR teams reminding him about the movie premiere. Invitations to events with people he barely knew.

Everything was moving fast. **Too fast.**

And still—

Still, he hesitated when he saw her name.

Lily.

He hadn't texted her in a year.

He had no reason to now.

He didn't know **where she was.**
What she was doing.
If she was even thinking about him at all.

And maybe that was a good thing.

Maybe she had finally **let go.**

Just like he was supposed to.

But as he locked his phone and stared at the flashing city lights outside his car window—

The feeling of **something unfinished** still didn't leave.

Lily stared at her desk, her pencil hovering over an empty page.

The art studio was **quiet**, filled with nothing but the faint scratching of brushes, the occasional murmur of students discussing their work.

Her mind, however, was **somewhere else.**

She had deleted the group chat.

Erased the last traces of what **used to be.**

And yet—why did it still feel like something was **pulling her back?**

She exhaled, shaking her head.

Focus. **Move forward.**

Then—

A voice.

**"Hi. Remember me?"**

Lily looked up.

A guy had taken the seat across from her, arms folded, a small smirk playing on his lips.

And the moment she saw him—

Her heart **stopped.**

It was him.

The stranger from the **art exhibition.**


She blinked, still processing. "You—?"

The guy chuckled. "So, you do remember me."

Lily sat up a little, trying to gather her thoughts. "I—yeah. I do. But…" She hesitated. "Are you… also in this college?"

He leaned back in his chair, nodding. "Just joined a few weeks ago. So technically…" He gave a small shrug. "I'm your junior."

Lily stared.

Out of all the things she had expected today, **this was not one of them.**

He was here.

In her college.

As her **junior.**

Her brain struggled to catch up. "That's… unexpected."

He grinned. "Good unexpected or bad unexpected?"

Lily hesitated. Then, softly—"Not sure yet."

That made him laugh.

It was light. **Easy.**

Like this wasn't **completely surreal.**

Like he had no idea what was about to hit her next.

Because the second she shook off her shock, something clicked in her brain—

And suddenly, she found herself asking, **without thinking—**

"What's your name?"

The guy raised an eyebrow, amused. "We talked twice, and you never asked?"

Lily pursed her lips. "I forgot."

He chuckled, then leaned forward slightly, resting his arms on the desk.

**"Kevin."**

The name hung in the air for half a second.

And then—

It hit her like a storm.

**Kevin?**

Kevin.

Kevin from the **arcade.**

Her breath caught.

Her hands clenched slightly.

**Oh my god.**

She **knew** him.

Lily's breath caught.

Her mind raced **backward**, piecing together fragments of a **memory she hadn't touched in years.**

Kevin.

Kevin from the **arcade.**

The dim neon lights.
The sound of tokens clinking.
The quiet smirk of a boy who hit her by mistake

And now?

He was sitting **right in front of her.**

Like it was the most **normal thing in the world.**


Kevin tilted his head slightly, watching her reaction.

"You okay?" he asked, his voice smooth—**too calm.**

Lily swallowed, her fingers tightening slightly on her sketchbook.

"…Kevin," she repeated, like saying it out loud would somehow make it **less shocking.**

He smirked. "That's me."

Lily's heart **pounded.**

Her mind was spinning, but he?

He looked **completely at ease.**

Like this was **normal.**

Like he had **expected this.**

"…We've met before," Lily finally said, her voice quieter now.

Kevin **held her gaze.**

Then, ever so slightly—**he smiled.**

"I know."

Something about the way he said it—calm, sure, knowing—sent a shiver down her spine.


Lily still couldn't **wrap her head around it.**

The same Kevin from the arcade.

The same Kevin who had disappeared just as easily as he had appeared back then.

And now—he was here.

**Why?**

How?

And more importantly—**why now?**

Before she could ask, Kevin leaned back slightly, resting his chin on his hand.

 "You never changed," he mused.

Lily blinked. "What?"

He gestured vaguely at her sketchbook.

Lily **stiffened.**

Because **how did he know that?**

They hadn't even talked to each other after that incident.

And yet—he was looking at her like he had known her **all along.**

Like he had been **waiting for this moment.**

Lily's grip tightened around her pencil.

**Something about this felt… off.**

Not in a **bad way.**

But in a way that made her **heart race. Oh definitely not a crush**

Kevin smirked again, like he could see right through her thoughts.

"Relax," he said smoothly. "I'm just here for college."

Why would he even say that? I didn't think of anything else though BUT

His voice was light. **Casual.**

But for some reason—**Lily didn't believe him.**

# 17.Spotlights & Shadows

Caleb adjusted his suit, staring at his reflection in the dressing room mirror.

The press event was about to start.

The cameras, the flashing lights, the interviews—**all of it.**

It was the kind of moment he had **once dreamed of.**

But now that he was here?

He felt **nothing.**


The event hall was **packed.**

Reporters, journalists, cameras flashing every second, the murmur of voices mixing with the occasional shout of excitement.

His co-stars moved through the crowd effortlessly, shaking hands, smiling for the cameras.

Caleb?

He just followed the motions.

**Pose. Smile. Speak. Repeat.**

He gave the right answers. Spoke about the film. Let people praise his performance.

And yet—

Even as the world **watched him**—

He had never felt more **invisible.**

Lily **didn't know what to make of Kevin.**

Ever since their unexpected reunion, he had **kept his distance**—but not really.

Somehow, **he was always there.**

A passing glance in the hallways.
A casual remark that made her **roll her eyes.**
The way he always **noticed things she wasn't saying.**

And the worst part?

She **let it happen.**

Even though she told herself she wouldn't.

Even though she knew better.

It wasn't **real** flirting. Not the kind that meant anything.

But it was **something.**

And for now?

That was **enough.**

Kevin sat across from her in the art studio, arms folded, **watching her sketch.**

"Are you always this serious when you draw?" he mused.

Lily didn't look up. "Are you always this distracting?"

Kevin smirked. "You haven't told me to leave yet."

She paused.

He wasn't wrong.

But instead of answering, she just **tilted her head slightly**, pretending to focus on her work.

Kevin leaned forward slightly, resting his chin on his hand.

"You know," he said, voice low, "if you keep avoiding eye contact, I might think you're shy."

Lily's pencil **halted.**

Her **face heated up.**

Slowly, she lifted her gaze, meeting his eyes **for exactly two seconds** before looking away again

Kevin chuckled.

Lily **scowled, throwing her eraser at him.**

"Shut up."

But Kevin?

Kevin just **grinned**, catching the eraser effortlessly.

Like he was enjoying this game.

Like he knew she was, too.

But that was all it was—**a game.**

Because no matter how easily their words **danced between them**—

Neither of them were willing to step **any closer.**


Kevin leaned back in his chair, watching her sketch with that usual **unreadable expression.**

Then, casually—

"Wanna get coffee?"

Lily glanced up.

Kevin smirked. "I know this amazing café."

For a second, she hesitated.

Then, before she could overthink it—

"Sure."

Kevin's smirk didn't falter.

He simply stood, stretching his arms. "Cool. The next week, after class?"

Lily nodded. "Okay."

And just like that—

They had plans.

The press event was **predictable.**

Caleb knew the drill.

Smile. Answer questions. **Smile again.**

"How is the movie going so far?"

"It's been an amazing experience. The cast and crew are incredible."

"When is the official release date?"

"Sometime next summer. We'll be announcing it soon."

But as he spoke, his gaze **caught onto something unusual in the crowd.**

A man.

Dressed in a **brown hat and suit**, the kind of old-fashioned look that didn't quite fit in here.

Something about him felt... **out of place.**

Caleb's gaze lingered for half a second—

Then, he brushed it off.

Just another face in the crowd.

Right?

After the event, Caleb exhaled, stepping backstage.

Finally.

A break.

He grabbed a water bottle, running a hand through his hair when—

A voice.

"Caleb Miller?"

Caleb turned.

And **froze.**

It was **him.**

The man from the crowd.

Up close, he looked even more **out of place**—but his stance was confident, like he belonged everywhere.

"Who's asking?" Caleb said carefully.

The man smiled, tipping his hat slightly.

"Name's **Tom Whitaker.** I represent **LK Music Company.**"

Caleb blinked. **LK Music?**

That was... **big.**

Before he could process, the man continued.

"We're looking to build a boy band." He paused, eyes sharp. "And we want you as the main vocal."

Caleb's breath caught.

**What?**

His dream.

The thing he had wanted **since forever.**

The man pulled out a **business card**, sliding it toward him.

"Think it over, kid. This could be your shot."

Then, just like that—

He turned and walked away.

Caleb stared at the card in his hand, his pulse **loud in his ears.**

A movie. A band.

Two different paths.

And for the second time in his life—

He had to choose.

Caleb sat in his dressing room, the **business card burning in his hands.**

LK Music.
A boy band.
Main vocal.

It was everything he had ever wanted—**so why was he hesitating?**

Before he could think too much, a **knock** sounded at the door.

Caleb frowned.

It wouldn't be his manager. They never knocked.

"Come in," he said, expecting—**well, he wasn't sure what.**

The door opened.

And Caleb **froze.**

Because the person standing there was **not James. Not Lily. Not anyone from his past.**

It was someone else.

And the moment their eyes met, Caleb knew—

This wasn't going to be **just another conversation.**

The door swung open.

Caleb expected a **manager, a co-star, maybe even a
journalist who had slipped past security.**

But instead—

A man stepped in.

Not old, not young. Mid-thirties, maybe. Dressed in **a
sleek black coat, polished shoes, and an air of quiet
confidence.**

His face was unfamiliar.

But something about him felt… **off.**

Like he wasn't just **passing through.**

Like he was here for a **reason.**

Caleb's fingers curled around the **business card in his
hand.**

The man's gaze flickered to it.

Then—**he smiled.**

**"LK Music, huh?"**

Caleb tensed slightly. "Who are you?"

The man stepped inside, letting the door close behind him.

**"Someone who knows exactly what you're about to
do."**

Caleb narrowed his eyes. **"And that is?"**

The man tilted his head.

"Make a choice you might regret."



Caleb set the card down carefully on the table, his eyes never leaving the man.

"Okay. You've got my attention." He leaned back. "Who sent you?"

The man chuckled, slipping his hands into his pockets.

"No one. I'm here on my own."

That didn't make Caleb feel any better.

Still, he kept his voice calm. "And why exactly do you care what I choose?"

The man sighed, like he had been **through this before.**

Then, he pulled something out of his pocket and slid it onto the table—

**A different business card.**

Caleb's eyes flicked down.

No flashy logos.

No gold lettering like LK Music's card.

Just a plain, black card with one thing printed on it.

A name.

And the moment Caleb read it, something in his chest **tightened.**

Because he knew that name.

Not personally.

But in the industry?

It was one that came with **whispers.**

Rumors.

Things people didn't say too loud.

Caleb **swallowed.**

The man smiled.

**"Now that you know who I am… let's talk about your future."**

Caleb's fingers **hovered** over the black business card.

The name on it felt **heavier than it should have.**

Not just a name—**a reputation.**

Something whispered in the backrooms of the industry.

Something **not talked about openly.**

Slowly, he looked up.

The man was still watching him, his smile **calm but unreadable.**

**"You're hesitating,"** he said, tilting his head slightly.

Caleb exhaled, his jaw tightening. **"You still haven't told me who you really are."**

The man smirked. **"Haven't I?"**

His tone was light, **but there was weight behind it.**

Caleb stared at the card again.

No company name. No details.

Just a name.

And that was **enough.**

Because **this wasn't just another record label.**

This wasn't LK Music, with their polished boy bands and chart-topping hits.

This was something **else.**

Something **bigger.**

Something **riskier.**


The man took a step forward, leaning slightly on the table.

**"You don't strike me as someone who wants to be just another name in a group."**

Caleb's breath hitched.

Because that was exactly what had been **bothering him.**

A boy band.

It was **his dream.** But in a way, it also **wasn't.**

He had always wanted music—**but his music.**

Not **something manufactured.**

Not something **temporary.**

The man watched his reaction carefully.

Then, as if reading his thoughts, he said—

**"You don't want to be a face in a crowd, Caleb. You want to be the name people remember."**

Silence.

Then—**softly, carefully—**

**"…And you're saying you can give me that?"**

The man smiled.

And this time, it wasn't just a smirk.

It was a **promise.**

**"I'm saying I can make you something bigger than you ever imagined."**

Caleb's heartbeat **pounded in his ears.**

LK Music. The safe choice. The predictable one.

Or this.

The unknown. The risk.

And maybe—**the chance to finally be something more.**

The man stepped back, nodding toward the card.

**"Think about it."**

Then, without another word—

He turned and walked out, leaving Caleb alone with a decision that could **change everything.**

Caleb stared at the black business card for what felt like **hours.**

The man's words echoed in his head.

**"You want to be the name people remember."**

A boy band?

Or something bigger?

He should've been **excited.**

Instead, he felt like he was **standing at the edge of something dangerous.**

Something he **didn't fully understand.**

He tried calling the number on the card **once.**

No answer.

He tried again a few days later.

Still nothing.

The man who had spoken to him with so much **certainty** had vanished just as quickly as he had appeared.

No online presence.
No company name attached to his offers.
Nothing.

It was as if he had been **a ghost.**

Caleb wasn't sure whether to feel **relieved or unsettled.**


Caleb had almost convinced himself that it was **just some scam.**

That maybe the man **wasn't as important as he seemed.**

But then, at an industry event, he overheard a conversation.

Someone mentioning a **big-time artist who had disappeared overnight.**

No scandal. No accident.

Just... **gone.**

The whisper of a **pattern.**

Something Caleb couldn't quite **grasp.**

And just like that—

He stopped looking for answers.

Maybe it was better that way.

Maybe some doors were **never meant to be opened.**



The calls came **fast.**

Record labels, producers, agencies—**all wanting a piece of him.**

His name had exploded after the movie.

His voice. His performance.

**Everyone wanted him.**

But Caleb already **knew** where he was going.

**LK Music.**

The offer had been there all along.

And now?

Now, he was **taking it.**

The contract was signed.

The papers sealed.

Caleb Miller—**officially in a boy band of six.**

He met them one by one.

Some older, some younger.

Some confident, some quiet.

But all of them had the same **hunger** in their eyes.

The hunger to **make it.**

To be **something bigger than just another name in the industry.**

And for the first time in a long time—

Caleb felt like he was finally **where he was meant to be.**


**Caleb Miller.** The main vocalist. The one with the voice that made people stop and listen.

And then—his new bandmates.

---

## 1. Ryan Lee – The Leader

A guy in his mid-20s, sharp-minded and **serious about business.** He wasn't the loudest, but when he spoke, people listened. **The foundation of the group.**

## 2. Ethan Park – The Performer

Charismatic, bold, and always stealing the spotlight. He had that **stage presence** that made crowds go insane. **Dancer, rapper, and pure energy.**

## 3. Noah Carter – The Songwriter

The quietest of them all, but his lyrics spoke louder than words. He had a **soft voice, a deep mind, and a way with melodies** that made every song hit different.

## 4. Zayn Malik – The Free Spirit

Not actually Malik, but he gave off those vibes. **Mysterious, laid-back, and effortlessly cool.** Played the guitar like it was a part of him.

## 5. Adrian Torres – The Youngest

The one with the **boyish charm,** always teasing but **never crossing the line.** His voice was sweet, his energy addicting. The type who'd annoy you and then make you laugh two seconds later.

Caleb sat in their practice room, looking at them—**his new brothers.**

This was it.

No turning back.

Their debut was in the works.

And for the first time in a long time—

Caleb wasn't alone.

# 18."Meanwhile, Lily…"

Lily hadn't seen Caleb's name in a while.

She had trained herself **not to look for it.**

Not in articles, not in industry news, not even when someone casually mentioned the **movie that made him famous.**

But avoiding his name didn't mean **forgetting him.**

And that was the part she hated the most.


Her professors loved her work.

They praised her **attention to detail**, the way she captured emotion, the depth in her strokes.

But Lily felt **nothing.**

She used to **love art.**

It was supposed to be **her escape.**

Now, it was just another **routine.**

A thing she did.
A thing she was *good* at.
A thing that was **supposed** to make her happy.

But at the end of the day, when she put down her brush—

She was still alone.

No Sophie. No James.

And Caleb?

Caleb was too far gone to even be **a memory.**

Lily walked beside Kevin, their conversation light, almost meaningless.

It wasn't **flirting**, not really.
Just **something to fill the silence.**

The café was a block away, the street buzzing with life.

And then—

She saw it.

A **massive LED screen**, mounted on the side of a building.

The opening shot—**six silhouettes.**

A deep bass. A slow fade-in.

Then, the logo at the bottom—

**LK Music.**

Lily **would've kept walking.**

She had trained herself **not to look.**

But then—

The camera panned.

And suddenly—**him.**


**Caleb.**

Standing in the center.
Singing.
Moving like he was born to be there.

Like he had finally become **everything he was meant to be.**

Lily's breath hitched.

Her steps slowed.

The world around her **blurred.**

She didn't even realize she had **stopped walking** until Kevin did too.

"…Lily?"

She didn't answer.

She couldn't.

The teaser ended.
The logo faded.

And the world?

It **kept moving.**

But Lily?

She just stood there.

Because after all this time, after everything—

She still **wasn't over it.**



He must feel the same too?

Right?

*Right?*



Kevin tilted his head slightly, following her gaze. "You okay?"

Lily blinked, snapping out of it. She forced herself to look away, tucking a strand of hair behind her ear. "Yeah. Just—" She cleared her throat. "Nothing."

Kevin didn't buy it. His eyes flicked back to the screen, watching the teaser replay. "Huh… weird."

Lily swallowed. "What?"

Kevin shrugged, stuffing his hands into his pockets. "That guy—the singer. He looks familiar." He turned to her, eyes narrowing slightly, as if piecing something together. "You sure you don't know him?"

Lily hesitated, gripping her phone tighter. "…I did."

Kevin studied her for a moment, the smirk fading just slightly before it returned—lazy, knowing. "That explains the whole 'stuck in place' moment."

Lily exhaled sharply, rolling her eyes. "Shut up."

His smirk widened. "Hey, I didn't say it was a bad thing. Just… interesting."

She ignored him, starting to walk again. "Let's just get coffee."

Kevin fell into step beside her, glancing at the screen one last time before looking forward. "Whatever," he said, his voice light. "It's none of my business, anyway."

But something about the way he said it—too casual, too easy—told her that he wasn't letting it go.

The café door had barely closed behind them when Kevin's phone buzzed.

Lily glanced at him, expecting him to silence it like before. But this time, he didn't.

Instead, he stared at the screen for a moment—too long, too still—before picking up.

Lily couldn't hear the other end of the conversation, but she saw it.

The way Kevin's jaw tensed. The way his fingers curled tighter around the phone.

Then—without a word—he turned and bolted out the door.

Lily blinked. "Kevin?"

He didn't stop.

Didn't even hesitate.

Panic flared in her chest as she hurried after him. "Kevin! Where are you going?"

Still, nothing.

His pace only quickened, his feet slamming against the pavement as if he was running out of time.

Lily hesitated for half a second before running too, her breath hitching in the cold air.

By the time she caught sight of him again, he was already at the main street, waving frantically for a cab.

The moment one stopped, he jumped in.

Lily barely had time to register what was happening before her phone rang.

Kevin.

She picked up immediately. "Kevin, what the hell—"

"I have to go." His voice was rushed, strained. In the background, she heard the crackle of a station announcement.

A train station?

"What? Go where?"

"I just—I had to leave," Kevin said. His breath was uneven, like he was trying to keep himself together. "I'll explain later."

Lily exhaled sharply, frustration and worry mixing in her chest. "Kevin, you literally just ran out—what's going on?"

Silence.

Then—

"I'll call you when I can."

Click.

The line went dead.

Lily lowered her phone, heart pounding.

Her breath curled in the cold air as she stood there, staring at the street.

Whatever just happened—

It wasn't normal.

Kevin never called back.

Not that day. Not the next.

Lily waited—checked her phone more times than she cared to admit—but the silence stretched on.

And then, nearly a week later, a message.

**"I'm in Texas."**

Just that. Nothing else.

Lily stared at the text, fingers hovering over her keyboard. Before she could type anything, another message came in.

**"She's gone."**

Her chest tightened.

She.

It didn't take much to put it together.

Kevin's mother—his sick mother, the one he had never spoken about in detail, the one he always brushed off with vague mentions of "she's managing" whenever Lily asked—was gone.

She exhaled, sitting back in her chair.

He had left Boston that night. Rushed to the station, boarded a train without looking back. Because Texas wasn't just a place—it was home.

And now, home wasn't the same anymore.

She wanted to say something.

**"I'm sorry."**

**"Are you okay?"**

**"Do you want to talk?"**

She typed. Deleted. Typed again.

In the end, all she sent was—

**"Kevin."**

The read receipt popped up almost instantly.

But no reply came.

Lily's phone buzzed again.

Another message from Kevin.

**"I think I'm gonna have to be here now."**

She read it once. Then again.

Something about those words felt final.

Like he wasn't just talking about staying in Texas for a little while. Like he was already settling into the idea of never coming back.

Lily swallowed, staring at the message.

She could picture it—Kevin in some quiet Texas town, standing outside a house that didn't feel the same anymore, surrounded by memories that had nowhere to go now.

Her fingers hovered over the keyboard.

**"Oh."**

No, too distant.

**"Are you sure?"**

Too dumb.

She exhaled, then finally typed:

**"You don't have to be alone, you know."**

Read. No reply.

Lily locked her phone and set it face down on the table.

She already knew.

Kevin wasn't coming back.

Another guy, gone.

Lily leaned back in her chair, staring at the ceiling.

First Caleb. Now Kevin.

It was funny, in a twisted kind of way. How people just—
left. How she kept getting used to it.

She told herself it didn't matter. That Kevin wasn't even
that close. That it wasn't the same.

But the hollow feeling in her chest said otherwise.

She picked up her phone again, scrolling through old
messages. Kevin's texts. Caleb's texts. Sophie's. James's.

All of them fading into silence.

Lily exhaled sharply, shutting her phone off.

Maybe this was just how things went.

People left and their loved ones too.


you just had to keep going.

The city was louder tonight.

Lily didn't know if it was her mind playing tricks on her or if everything really was moving faster, brighter, more alive. The streets, the neon signs, the people laughing in the distance—it was like the world was rushing forward, leaving her behind.

She pulled her jacket closer, walking without really knowing where she was going.

And then—

She walked straight into someone.

"Oh—sorry," she mumbled, snapping out of her daze.

The stranger adjusting his hoodie. "Oh my bad."

And just like that, they both kept walking. Like two drifting souls passing by, never to meet again.

**The Next Day**

The examination hall was cold. Too cold.

Lily sat at her desk, tapping her pen against the paper. This was it. **The exam that determined her career.**

She should've felt nervous.

She should've been scared out of her mind.

But all she could think about was Caleb.

How he had it all figured out. How he had been given an opportunity, and he took it without hesitation.

She let out a quiet laugh, shaking her head as she flipped through the questions.

**No preparation. No plan. No fear.**

She didn't even know why she was here.

Still, she started writing.

**Two Days Later**

Lily walked anxiously through the halls of her apartment, her hands clammy.

Regret. **So much regret.**

Why did she go in so unprepared?

Why did she treat the most important test of her life like it was just another school quiz?

The sound of an email notification snapped her out of it.

Her laptop screen glowed in the dim room.

**Results.**

Her heart pounded as she typed in her ID and roll number, her fingers slightly trembling.

The screen loaded.

**296/300.**

A+.

Lily's breath hitched.

She blinked. Once. Twice.

Her eyes darted to the job opportunities rolling down the page. **Art studios. Graphic design firms. Animation companies.**

She felt… weird.

Excited. Overwhelmed. Shocked.

**Was this real?**

A sharp laugh escaped her lips—half disbelief, half something she didn't know how to name.

And before she even realized what she was doing, she ran.

Down the stairs. Out of the building.

The cold breeze hit her like a wave, cooling her burning cheeks.

She stood in the middle of the street, under the flickering streetlights, hands on her knees as she caught her breath.

**She did it.**

The stranger was caleb.

Seen yet unseen huh?

# 19. The Spotlight and the Silence

Lily sat on the rooftop of her apartment, legs tucked under her, staring at the city lights stretching endlessly before her.

The world below was alive—cars honking, music playing from some distant bar, laughter spilling into the night air.

She should've felt the same. **Alive. Accomplished. Excited.**

But all she felt was... empty.

**She had done it.** The exam she walked into blindly, the one she thought she failed? She aced it. Opportunities lined up for her, doors wide open, the future waiting.

So why did it feel like she was still standing at the beginning of something unknown?

She picked at the hem of her sweater. Maybe it was because she had no one to share it with.

James would've made some dumb joke about how she "accidentally became a genius."
Sophie would've forced her to celebrate, dragging her to some party.
And Caleb—

Lily sighed, tilting her head back.

**Caleb.**

That name still echoed in her mind like a song stuck on repeat.

The boy who had disappeared into the world of music, becoming everything he had ever wanted to be.

**Did he even remember her?**

She squeezed her eyes shut. No. **No, she wasn't going to think about that.**

**Not now.**

Not when she finally had something of her own.

The lights blinded Caleb as he stood on stage. The cameras clicked, the audience cheered, the energy of the room buzzing in his ears.

The interviewer smiled at him, microphone close. "So, Caleb, tell us—how does it feel? Your debut song is already topping charts, the world is falling in love with your voice. Is this everything you imagined?"

Caleb smiled. Said the things he knew he was supposed to say.

"It's incredible. A dream come true."

The crowd erupted into applause.

But somewhere, deep in his chest, an ache lingered.

It wasn't the stage. It wasn't the cameras. It wasn't the attention.

It was something else. **Something missing.**

As the interview continued, his eyes drifted for a second—just a second—toward the giant LED screen behind them.

A clip from their music video played. Him and the five other members. Their voices blending in harmony.

He should've been focused on the present. On the dream unfolding before him.

But all he could think about—

**Was the girl who used to listen when no one else did.**


Lily sat at her desk, her laptop screen glowing in the dim room. The list of jobs scrolled endlessly, opportunities stretching out before her like roads she could take.

She exhaled sharply, leaning back in her chair. **Graphic designer.**

It clicked.

The way colors, shapes, and emotions could blend into something powerful. The way an idea could come to life through design.

It made sense.

She wasn't just picking a career. She was picking **her future**.

Lily sat up straighter, fingers hovering over the keyboard.

**This was it.**

With a deep breath, she clicked **"Apply."**

And just like that—her path was set.

The black van cruised through the city streets, headlights cutting through the night. Inside, the atmosphere was a mix of exhaustion and casual conversation—except for Caleb, who sat quietly by the window, lost in thought.

Ryan smirked, arms crossed as he leaned back against his seat. "A girl, huh?"

Caleb's gaze flickered to him, caught off guard. "What?"

Ryan chuckled. "You've been acting weird since the press event. It's gotta be about a girl."

Ethan laughed, nudging Theo. "Told you, man. It's always the quiet ones."

Theo grinned. "So? Spill. Who is she?"

Caleb shook his head, exhaling. "It's nothing."

Ryan scoffed. "Yeah, sure. That's why you've been staring out the window like a lost puppy."

The others chuckled, but Zayn, who had been quiet until now, leaned forward. "Well, whatever it is, you better snap out of it."

Caleb glanced at him, raising an eyebrow.

Zayn smirked. "You do remember the party tomorrow, right? All the big names are gonna be there. Renowned celebs, top artists—basically, the people who could change your whole career. So cheer up, man."

Caleb sighed, running a hand through his hair. He knew Zayn was right. This was a big deal.

And yet, his mind wasn't on the party at all.

The morning air was crisp as Lily stepped into **DSN Graphic Design Company**, her heart buzzing with excitement and nerves. The moment she walked in, she felt something she hadn't in a long time—belonging.

She was introduced to her partners, each shaking her hand and welcoming her with friendly smiles. But one person stood out—**June**.

June had short, dyed blue hair, round glasses, and a confident smirk. "New here?"

Lily nodded. "Yeah. First day."

"Well, good luck. The bosses aren't the worst, but deadlines will make you question your existence," June joked, nudging her.

Lily laughed, instantly liking her. "Noted."

As the hours passed, they worked side by side, brainstorming, sketching, bringing ideas to life. By lunch, they had already clicked.

At the cafeteria, June sat across from Lily, taking a bite of her sandwich. "So, what's your story? Always wanted to do design?"

Lily thought for a moment. "I guess I did. I just… never really thought I'd get here."

June smirked. "Well, you did. And you're good at it."

Lily smiled. It had been so long since someone had said something like that to her.

The workday flew by, and as Lily walked home, she thought, **At least I have someone.**

The atmosphere was electric. Celebrities, producers, directors—everyone who mattered in the entertainment industry was there.

Caleb had spent most of the night in conversations—big names from the music industry, co-actors from his musical movie. It should've been exciting. A dream.

But his mind kept drifting.

Still, he shook hands, nodded, smiled—played his part.

Then, the moment arrived.

Caleb returned to his band, and in front of flashing cameras and a roaring crowd, **they finally revealed their band name.**

**ECLIPSE.**

The audience erupted in applause. It was official. This was it.

And then—

Zayn collapsed.

Gasps filled the room as people rushed toward him.

"Someone call an ambulance!"

Ryan was already kneeling beside him, shaking him slightly. "Zayn! Zayn, wake up!"

Panic. Confusion. Fear.

The medics arrived, lifting him onto the stretcher.

"I'm sorry," Ryan whispered, his hands shaking


Hours later.

A hospital room. Silence thick as smoke.

Then the doctor's voice.

"We failed him"

No heck of a way

**"We found traces of Ambien in his system. A strong dosage."**

Ryan paled. "What?"

The doctor hesitated. "Someone could have spiked his drink."

Shock. Horror.

Ryan clenched his fists. "No. No way. Zayn wouldn't—he never had trouble sleeping. He wouldn't take sleeping pills."

Caleb stood frozen, feeling his stomach twist. This wasn't happening. This couldn't be happening.

Then—

**The news broke.**

Billboards. Headlines. TV screens.

**"ZAYN MALIK OF ECLIPSE KILLED BY A HIGH DOSAGE OF AMBIEN."**

Speculation ran wild.

**"Murder?"**
**"Accidental overdose?"**
**"Who did this?"**

Ryan lost it. He **broke down**, his entire body trembling.
Caleb wasn't far behind.

This was supposed to be their night. Their beginning.

Instead—

It became a nightmare.

# 20. The Investigation begins

The world had changed overnight.

What was supposed to be the grand debut of **Eclipse** had turned into a **crime scene**.

The air was heavy with silence as police sirens blared outside the hospital where **Zayn Malik** had been taken, only for doctors to confirm what the world feared.

**Zayn was gone.**

The reporters outside the building yelled for statements. Fans flooded the internet with messages of disbelief. **#JusticeForZayn** trended worldwide.

But inside, within the cold, sterile walls of the police station, the remaining members of Eclipse sat, shaken, exhausted, and silent.

Caleb hadn't spoken a word since they had arrived.

Ryan sat with his head in his hands, gripping his hair so tightly his knuckles turned white.

"I should've been there," he whispered, his voice hollow. "I should've stopped him. I should've—"

"You couldn't have known," Jay cut in, but his voice lacked conviction.

**The truth was, none of them knew.**

None of them had noticed the signs.

None of them had seen Zayn struggling—because was he struggling?

That was the part that didn't make sense.

Zayn wasn't reckless. He wasn't self-destructive. He didn't have any medical conditions that they knew of. He had never once mentioned trouble sleeping, let alone taking sleeping pills.

So how did Ambien get into his system?

The officer sitting across from them leaned forward. "We need to know exactly what happened. Walk us through the party."

They had arrived at **8 PM**, dressed in all black, walking onto the red carpet like stars. Cameras flashed. Fans screamed. Reporters crowded around, but the night had felt electric—exciting.

At **9:30 PM**, Zayn had been laughing. Smiling. Clinking glasses with fellow celebrities.

At **10:00 PM**, they revealed the name of their band: **Eclipse**.

At **10:07 PM, Zayn collapsed.**

**Seven minutes.**

That was all it took.

The police checked **security footage**. They zoomed in on **Zayn's glass of champagne.**

A bartender had handed it to him.

The officers tracked him down. **His name was Ethan Carter.**

For hours, they interrogated him, pressing him for details.

"Did you see anyone tamper with his drink?"

Ethan shook his head. "I didn't. I—I just serve drinks. I don't even remember who ordered that one."

He was nervous but not guilty.

Then—

A **breakthrough.**

Forensic results came in.

**Traces of Ambien were found on the rim of Zayn's glass.**

The champagne had been spiked.

The question was—**who did it?**

The security team scoured through hours of footage until they found it.

**A shadowy figure standing near the drinks table.**

Not interacting. Just **waiting.**

The person's face wasn't clear, but—

They were wearing a **gold ring with a distinct symbol.**

A chill ran down Caleb's spine.

**He had seen that ring before.**

But where?

Then, another lead emerged—Zayn's **phone records.**

There was a message sent to him before the party from an **unknown number.**

**Unknown Number:**
*Be careful tonight. You don't know who's watching.*

But Zayn had **never responded.**

And when the police traced the number—

**It was unregistered.**

Then, a **new name entered the investigation.**

A well-known **music producer.**

**Lucas Hayes.**

A man infamous for **scouting young talent**—and also for **being ruthless.**

The police dug deeper.

Lucas had approached Zayn earlier that night, offering him a **solo contract.**

Zayn had **refused.**

And hours later, he was **dead.**

The puzzle pieces started falling into place.

Lucas was brought in for questioning.

At first, he denied everything.

But then the police **showed him the security footage**—his hand brushing against Zayn's glass moments before the drink was served.

The **ring on his finger matched.**

Under pressure, he finally **confessed.**

But what he said made everyone freeze.

**"I didn't mean to kill him."**

The room went silent.

Lucas's hands trembled. "It was just a small dose. Just enough to make him feel sick. I thought… maybe he'd miss the debut. Maybe he'd reconsider my offer."

Ryan's eyes burned with fury. "You drugged him?"

Lucas swallowed hard. "I didn't think it would—"

"You didn't think?" Ryan snapped, standing so fast his chair clattered to the ground. "You thought screwing with his health would make him listen to you?"

Caleb grabbed Ryan's arm before he could lunge.

The officers didn't move. They didn't have to. The case was clear.

Lucas Hayes was charged with **manslaughter.**

**The Aftermath**

The world exploded with the news.

The headlines read:
**"Music Producer Lucas Hayes Arrested in Connection to Zayn Malik's Death."**
**"Murder or Manslaughter? The Dark Truth of the Industry."**
**"Eclipse's Debut Ruined by Tragedy."**

Fans were devastated.

The music industry was shaken.

And Eclipse?

**Eclipse was never the same again.**

Ryan withdrew from everything.

Jay stopped talking as much.

Caleb felt… **empty.**

One moment, they were celebrating their dream.

The next, they were **burying one of their own.**

And in the middle of it all, Caleb realized something.

**No matter how high you rise—no matter how far you go—some things, some people… you never truly leave behind.**

# 21.Silence In the Aftermath

The world **moved on.**

News cycles changed. The industry **buzzed with new headlines, new scandals, new faces.**

But for Eclipse—

For the five boys who had once stood together as six—

**Time had stopped.**

**The Weight of a Name**

Their band name, once meant to symbolize their rise, now felt **like a curse.**

*Eclipse.*

The day they had revealed their name to the world was **the same day they lost Zayn.**

Caleb still remembered **the weight of the microphone in his hand, the bright lights, the cameras flashing, the cheers of the crowd—**

And then—

Zayn collapsing.

The panic.

The chaos.

The sirens.

Ryan's hands shaking as he held onto Zayn, **begging him to wake up.**

The cold, sterile air of the hospital waiting room.

The doctor walking in with that look—the look that meant **it was over.**

The slow, shattering realization that Zayn wasn't coming back.

In the days that followed, everything **crumbled.**

Management **froze all activities.**

Eclipse was put on **indefinite hiatus.** No more rehearsals. No promotions. No comeback schedule.

Nothing.

It was like the band had **never existed.**

Ryan disappeared first. **He left the city.** No one knew where he went, but rumors spread—**he had checked into a private retreat, cutting off all contact.**

Jay shut himself in his apartment. **No messages, no calls, no sightings.**

Noah tried to **distract himself with work,** spending hours locked in the studio, but it was clear—he wasn't creating music. Just **drowning in silence.**

Ethan was the only one trying to **hold the pieces together.**

But even he was **cracking.**

And Caleb—

Caleb felt **nothing.**

He **stopped responding** to texts.

Stopped picking up the phone.

Stopped singing.

The voice that had once carried him through everything—his pain, his dreams, his ambitions—was now just… **silent.**

Because what was the point?

New artists debuted. New scandals surfaced.

Eclipse's **hiatus** became just another story in the archives.

**A rising star burned out too soon.**

That was all they had become.

And for the first time, Caleb realized—

Fame was temporary.

A single mistake, a single moment, **and you could disappear.**

Zayn had been proof of that.

**Lily Saw the News**

Lily had been in the middle of work when she saw the headline.

The bright LED screen in the office flashed with breaking news:

**"Eclipse Member Found Dead After Alleged Drug Incident."**

Her stomach dropped.

The air **left her lungs.**

She blinked at the screen, trying to process the words, but **they blurred together.**

Her hands trembled as she reached for her phone, **searching.**

More articles.

More details.

**Zayn.** Gone.

And Caleb—

His band **disbanded.**

She gripped her phone tightly, her heartbeat **loud in her ears.**

*Caleb.*

That name repeated in her head.

*Is he okay?*

*How is he handling this?*

She hadn't talked to him in **months.**

Hadn't checked in. Hadn't messaged.

They had all drifted, and she **hated it.**

Now, for the first time in so long, she wanted to hear his voice.

She opened his contact.

Her thumb hovered over the call button.

But she hesitated.

Would he even pick up?

Would he even want to talk to her?

She swallowed hard.

And then—

She locked her phone.

Because **deep down, she already knew the answer.**

*Nothing would ever be the same again.*


Lily thought "I jinxed it didn't I?"

If you know, you know

# 22. The city moves,but she stays

The city moved on without them.

Bright lights flashed. Cars honked. People laughed, shouted, **lived.**

But Lily?

Lily just stood there.

She leaned against the rusting metal pole of the bus stop, her bag slung over her shoulder, exhaustion settling into her bones. The day had been long—work had been draining—but nothing compared to the emptiness that settled in the spaces **no one else could see.**

She glanced at her phone. No messages. Not that she had been expecting any.

The wind was cool against her face, tugging at strands of her hair as she watched the cars rush by.

Somewhere, amidst the blur of moving lights and shifting shadows—

**He was out there.**

Caleb.

Moving through the city.

The same city, the same streets.

But still miles away.

**Elsewhere, Caleb walked.**

No destination, no purpose. Just him and the cold pavement beneath his sneakers.

Boston had always been too loud for him. Too many lights, too many people, too many reminders.

But tonight?

It was quieter.

Maybe because he wasn't really listening.

His hands were shoved deep into his pockets, his hood pulled over his head, as he let the streets guide him.

There was nowhere to go.

Or maybe—he just didn't want to go anywhere.

Not back to the empty hotel room. Not back to the silence.

His fingers twitched slightly. An old habit.

He used to reach for his phone when things got too heavy. **Back when there was someone to text.**

But now?

Now, there was no one.

Caleb exhaled, stepping into a crosswalk as headlights painted him in white and gold.

For a second, just a second, he thought about turning back.

Back to what, though?

The past was long gone.

And yet—

Somewhere, in this same city, she was there.

Lily.

Existing under the same sky.

Breathing the same air.

Maybe just **a street away.**

And somehow, that made all the difference.

The bus hissed as it came to a stop.

Lily barely registered it as she stepped on, swiping her card, finding a seat near the window. She wasn't really paying attention to anything—just staring at the blurry city lights flashing past.

It was just another night.

Just another bus ride home.

Until it wasn't.



Caleb stepped onto the bus without thinking.

He hadn't planned to take it—he had just been walking, letting the night pull him forward, when he saw it slowing down.

And for some reason, he got on.

Maybe it was exhaustion. Maybe it was fate.

Maybe it was something else entirely.

He moved past a few empty seats, his mind elsewhere, his fingers fidgeting slightly.

Then—

**Clink.**

Something hit his foot and rolled to a stop.

A water bottle.

He blinked, leaning down to pick it up—when he heard a familiar voice.

"Oh—I'm sorry, that's mine."

And that was the moment time stopped.

Caleb straightened, fingers tightening around the bottle as his gaze lifted—

**And there she was.**

Lily.

Sitting by the window, her eyes wide, the soft glow of the city catching in them.

For a second, neither of them moved.

Neither of them breathed.

Just silence, thick and heavy, stretching between them.

Lily's lips parted slightly, like she wanted to say something—but no words came out.

Caleb felt something strange in his chest, something tight and unfamiliar. He swallowed, finally remembering to **breathe.**

"…Lily?"

Her name tasted foreign on his tongue. Like something he hadn't said in years.

She nodded slowly, hesitantly. "Hey… Caleb."

His fingers loosened around the bottle. "I, uh… this is yours."

He held it out to her, and she reached forward to take it, her fingers brushing against his for just a second—

A second too long.

Something electric shot through him, but he quickly pulled his hand back, shoving it into his pocket.

Lily held the bottle, gripping it like it was an anchor. Her heart was **racing.**

"…It's been a while," she finally said.

Caleb nodded. "Yeah." His voice was quieter than he meant it to be.

Neither of them knew what to say next.

The bus moved forward. The city blurred outside the window.

And for the first time in a long time—

**They weren't strangers anymore.**


Caleb watched as Lily settled back into her seat after glancing out the window. The city lights flickered across her face, painting soft golden streaks over her features. There was something so **unreal** about this—sitting next to her, talking like the past few years hadn't unraveled the way they did.

He exhaled, running a hand through his hair. "You know… the group's finally out of hiatus."

Lily turned to him, eyes widening slightly. "Really?"

He nodded. "Yeah. It took some time after… after everything with Zayn. But we're back now."

Lily hesitated. "That must've been… hard."

Caleb didn't answer immediately. His fingers tapped against his knee, a habit he didn't even realize he still had. "It was. Losing him like that. It felt like the ground disappeared from under us."

Lily bit her lip. "I heard the news." She looked at him carefully. "I—I wanted to reach out."

Caleb turned to her, eyes locking onto hers. "Why didn't you?"

She inhaled sharply, looking away. "I don't know."

Another pause. The bus moved steadily forward, carrying them through the heart of the city.

Caleb watched her, searching her expression. "So, graphic design?"

Lily nodded, a small smile tugging at the corner of her lips. "Yeah. I started working at DSN a while ago. It's been… surprisingly good."

His eyebrows raised slightly. "You love it?"

"I do." She glanced at him. "It feels right, you know?"

Caleb's lips quirked upward. "Yeah. I get that."

Lily tilted her head slightly, studying him. "And you? Does being in the band feel right?"

Caleb let out a quiet chuckle, but there was something softer underneath it. "It does. I mean, it's not easy. There's a lot of pressure. A lot of expectations. But… yeah. It's what I wanted."

Lily smiled. "I'm glad."

Caleb hesitated, then added, "I think Zayn would've wanted us to keep going too."

Lily's smile faltered just a little. "I'm sure he would."

Silence settled between them again, but it wasn't awkward. It was something else. Something almost **comfortable.**

Then—

Caleb spoke again.

"You said something's missing."

Lily blinked, caught off guard.

Caleb's gaze was steady. "Earlier. You said you love what you do, but it still feels like something's missing."

She let out a slow breath, staring down at the water bottle in her hands. "I don't know what it is."

Caleb watched her carefully, then said, almost too softly—

"Maybe you do."

Lily's fingers curled around the bottle.

The bus began slowing down. **Her stop.**

She looked at him one last time, hesitating, before offering a small smile. "Maybe."

Then, as the bus came to a halt, she stood up.

The bus rumbled forward, the city outside a blur of neon and headlights. But inside, it was quieter—**just them.**

Lily didn't get off. Not yet.

She sat back down, hesitating for a second before finally asking, **"So… what happens now?"**

Caleb turned to her, confused. "What do you mean?"

She shrugged, fingers fidgeting with the cap of her water bottle. "I mean… are we just going to pretend we didn't disappear from each other's lives?"

Caleb looked at her for a long moment. Then, a small, almost sheepish smile crossed his face. **"I don't want to disappear again."**

Lily met his gaze, and something in her chest **tightened.**

She **didn't** want to disappear again either.

A small silence stretched between them, but this time, it wasn't **heavy.** It was something softer, lighter—like they had **found something again.**

Caleb exhaled, leaning back against his seat. **"We could… I don't know. Stay in touch?"**

Lily smirked. "You sound so confident about it."

Caleb chuckled, shaking his head. "I just—It's been a while. I don't know how this works anymore."

Lily smiled, a real one this time. "Then let's just figure it out."

Caleb looked at her again, really looked at her. And for the first time in years, he didn't feel like he was chasing after something just out of reach.

He **found it.**

He found **her.**

The bus slowed down at her stop.

Lily finally stood, but before stepping off, she turned back to him. "So…" She hesitated for a second before pulling out her phone. **"Give me your number."**

Caleb raised an eyebrow, amused. "You still don't have it?"

She rolled her eyes. "I deleted it a long time ago."

Caleb chuckled, shaking his head as he took her phone and typed in his number.

When he handed it back, their fingers brushed for the briefest second.

Lily's breath caught.

Caleb's heart **skipped.**

She looked at the screen. **Saved.**

Lily glanced at him one last time before stepping off the bus.

Caleb watched as she walked away, disappearing into the streets.

But this time, she wasn't gone.

This time, he knew—

They'd talk again.


As the bus slowed to a stop, Lily stood up, adjusting the strap of her bag. She turned back to Caleb, hesitating just for a second before offering him a soft, familiar smile—the kind that **felt like home.**

**"It was nice meeting you, Caleb,"** she said, her voice gentle, almost teasing.

And just like that, she stepped off the bus, disappearing into the night.

But Caleb? He stayed frozen in his seat, **staring after her.**

That smile.

That exact same smile.

**His mind blurred—flashing, spinning—dragging him back.**

**High school.**

A sunlit classroom, her sitting a few rows ahead of him, turning around after a debate in class, **grinning as she won the argument.**

The school hallway, after an exam, **that same victorious smirk** as she whispered, *"I totally aced that."*

The **sports competition,** the first time he ever saw her—standing at the finish line, hands on her knees, out of breath, but **smiling through it all.**

And then—**graduation day.**

Hats flying in the air. The crowd cheering. The end of everything.

Lily, across the sea of students, **meeting his gaze, mouthing the words,** *"It's all over."*

And yet—**here they were.**

Not over.

Not gone.

Not forgotten.

—

The doors of the bus closed. The engine rumbled as it pulled away, but Caleb? He was **still stuck in the past.**

Still stuck in the moment she had smiled at him.

Just like she used to.

Just like she always had.

He exhaled, running a hand through his hair.

He should've said something.

**Anything.**

But instead, he pulled out his phone.

Opened his contacts.

Scrolled until he found her name—**Lily.**

And for the first time in years, he had something he never thought he'd have again.

A second chance.

# 23.Coffee at 4?

It had been a few days.

A few days since the bus. Since that moment. Since the past and present blurred into something neither of them were ready for.

Lily wasn't sure why she kept thinking about it.

Maybe it was the way Caleb had looked at her—like he had seen a ghost. Maybe it was how, even after all this time, talking to him felt like walking on a tightrope, unsure if she'd slip or if he'd catch her. Maybe it was just **nostalgia.**

But she had convinced herself that was all it was.

Her life had changed. So had his.

And yet—

When her phone buzzed, a message lighting up the screen, her heart still skipped a beat.

**"Coffee at 4?"**

She stared at it for a second. Then another.

It was simple. Casual.

But it wasn't.

Not when it was **him.**

Her fingers hovered over the keyboard before she finally typed back.

**"Sure."**

She hit send.

Somewhere across the city, Caleb exhaled, leaning back against his couch, staring at the message like it held something heavier than it should.

Just coffee.

That's all it was.

So why did it feel like something more?

The studio felt different.

Caleb sat at the piano, fingers hovering over the keys, the soft glow of the recording booth casting long shadows. The air was thick with something unspoken, something unfinished.

Ryan sat cross-legged on the couch, head resting against the armrest, lazily tapping his fingers against his knee. Adrian, leaning against the console, rolled a pen between his fingers, lost in thought.

But Caleb?

He was lost in a memory.

A **bus stop.**

A **message.**

A **smile.**

"Alright," Ryan muttered, breaking the silence. "We need something real for this track."

Adrian nodded. "Something that stays."

Caleb exhaled, flipping to a blank page in his notebook.

And then—he started writing.

**A song that wouldn't just be heard.**
**A song that would stay.**

Hours passed.

The song took shape—piece by piece, word by word, memory by memory.

Ryan hummed the chorus under his breath. "This one feels… different."

Adrian glanced at Caleb. "It's a confession, isn't it?"

Caleb didn't answer.

Instead, his gaze fell to two lines on the page, the ink still fresh—

**"Somewhere between hello and goodbye,
We lost the words but never the time."**

A breath.

A realization.

This wasn't just a song.

This was a moment.

One that hadn't ended.

Adrian smirked. "So what's the title?"

Caleb tapped his pen against the paper, then—finally—wrote it down.

**"Always, Almost."**

Ryan raised an eyebrow. "That's… deep."

Caleb smiled—just a little.

"It should be."

The café smelled of roasted beans and vanilla. Soft jazz hummed from the speakers, blending with the quiet chatter of people tucked into corners.

Lily sat at a small table near the window, fingers curled around a warm cup of coffee. She had arrived a little early, not that she'd admit it.

She had told herself this was just coffee. Just two people catching up.

But her heart didn't seem to get the memo.

The bell above the door jingled.

Lily glanced up.

And there he was.

Caleb.

His hair was slightly tousled, a few strands falling over his forehead. He spotted her almost instantly, his lips curving into something soft, something familiar.

"Hey," he said, sliding into the seat across from her.

"Hey," she echoed.

A pause. A glance. A shared silence that somehow wasn't uncomfortable.

Caleb rubbed the back of his neck, looking down at his coffee. "I, uh… wasn't sure if you'd come."

Lily tilted her head. "Why wouldn't I?"

He hesitated. Then, quieter—"I don't know. Guess I just thought… maybe too much time had passed."

Lily looked at him for a moment, then shook her head. "Not enough," she said softly.

Caleb met her gaze. And for the first time in a long time, it felt like the space between them wasn't filled with everything unspoken.

They talked—about work, about life, about how weird it felt to be adults now. Lily told him about her new job and her friendship with June. Caleb told her about his band, about Adrian and Ryan.

And then—

"I have something to show you," he said, pulling out his phone.

Lily blinked. "Okay…?"

He tapped on the screen, then slid the phone across the table.

A song title glowed on the screen.

**"Always, Almost."**

Lily's breath caught.

Caleb pressed play.

And as the first notes filled the air between them, her world slowed.

The melody was soft yet powerful, familiar yet brand new. And then his voice—his voice—spun the words into something alive.

**"Somewhere between hello and goodbye,
We lost the words but never the time."**

Lily didn't realize she was gripping the edges of the phone.

When the song ended, the café faded back into existence, but she was still lost in it.

She looked up at him. Eyes shining. Breath unsteady.

"Caleb…" she whispered.

His fingers drummed against his coffee cup. "Do you like it?"

Lily let out a breathless laugh. "I love it."

And in that moment, Caleb knew—

**She heard it.**

She knew.


"Wow, She's a special one huh?" She flipped through her cards and settled on one. "But it has been confirmed that you'll be taking a break from *Eclipse Crew* for about a year. That's huge news. Can you tell us why?"

The teasing air around Caleb shifted. The room seemed to lean in.

He swallowed, adjusting the mic clipped to his suit. Then, he ran a hand through his hair and let out a breath.

A pause.

Then—

**"I'm getting married."**

The silence was deafening.

The interviewer blinked. The audience gasped.

Then, chaos.

"Wait, wait—hold on!" The interviewer barely managed to suppress her excitement as the live chat on the broadcast exploded. "Caleb, are you serious?"

His lips curled into the smallest, most genuine smile. "Yeah. I am."

The room buzzed with whispers. The cameras zoomed in.

"Who's the lucky girl?"

He exhaled, his mind drifting to the one person who had always been there—before the fame, before the music, before *Eclipse Crew* even existed.

But instead of answering, he only grinned. "You'll find out soon enough."

The audience groaned in frustration, but it was too late. The interview was ending. Caleb stood up, shaking hands with the interviewer as the camera crew wrapped up.

And then—

It cut to black.

The hall shimmered beneath the glow of golden chandeliers, casting soft, flickering patterns across the sea of guests. White roses adorned every corner, their delicate scent weaving into the air, blending with the hushed murmurs and quiet anticipation.

At the altar, Caleb Miller stood, his hands loosely clasped in front of him, the weight of the moment pressing into his chest. He could hear the faint hum of the song— *Always, Almost*—playing softly in the background, the melody wrapping around him like a memory.

His heart pounded.

It wasn't like the usual pre-show jitters before stepping onto the stage. This was different. This wasn't about the cameras, the flashing lights, or the thousands of screaming fans.

This was *her*.

His life, his past, his future—standing at the end of the aisle.

The doors creaked open, and in the warm glow of the afternoon sun, she appeared.

A quiet hush fell over the hall.

Each step was slow, measured, almost hesitant, as if she herself couldn't believe this was real. The ivory lace of her gown cascaded down in soft waves, hugging her frame before flowing effortlessly with every step. The delicate veil draped over her face caught the light just enough to make her seem almost unreal.

Caleb exhaled shakily.

He had seen her in so many ways—flustered, annoyed, laughing, lost in thought—but this?

She looked breathtaking.

And yet, beneath the beauty of the moment, something tugged at him—a deep, unwavering realization.

He was marrying *her*.

The girl who once sat a few rows behind him on the bus.
The girl who unknowingly changed everything.
The girl he had spent years without—only to find her

again, as if fate had rewound the tape of their lives and hit *play* at the perfect moment.

His hands clenched slightly at his sides, his breath uneven as she moved closer.

Their eyes met.

A soft, knowing smile tugged at her lips—one he had seen a thousand times before, yet today, it felt different.

More real.

More *theirs*.

And just like that, she was in front of him.

Sophie and James stood to the side, grinning ear to ear. Ryan and Adrian exchanged glances, nodding to each other as if silently saying, *This is it*.

The officiant, an elderly man with kind eyes, stepped forward, smiling warmly at the two of them. He cleared his throat, and the hall fell into an expectant silence.

**"Caleb Miller, do you take _________ as your wife?"**

Caleb inhaled.

This was it.

For a moment, he thought about the boy he used to be— the boy who only ever sought perfection because it was drilled into him. The boy who had been so lost in a world of expectations that he forgot how to simply *live*.

And then, there was *her*.

The one who had unknowingly pulled him out of the void, without even trying.

His fingers twitched slightly as he forced himself to breathe.

His gaze flickered over to her—standing there, waiting.

Her lips parted ever so slightly, her chest rising and falling as if she, too, was holding her breath.

A thousand thoughts ran through his mind, but in the end, there was only one truth.

One answer.

**"Yes."**

A collective sigh of relief swept through the hall.

Somewhere in the crowd, Sophie wiped at her eyes. James nudged her playfully, whispering something that made her roll her eyes, though the tears in them gave her away.

Ryan clapped a hand on Adrian's shoulder, murmuring, "That's our boy."

But Caleb—he didn't hear any of it.

Because now, it was her turn.

The officiant turned to her, smiling softly.

**"Lily Parker, do you take Caleb Miller as your husband?"**

A pause.

Her lips parted slightly, her breath shaky.

It wasn't hesitation. No, not at all.

It was everything crashing down on her all at once.

The years of growing up, of watching everything fall apart
and come back together.
The friendships, the late-night conversations, the *almosts*
that turned into *nevers*.
The messages that had once been so constant, only to
stop—until they started again.

She blinked.

Caleb was watching her.

She could feel the weight of his gaze, the nervous energy
radiating from him.

For a second, she wanted to laugh.

This was Caleb—*her* Caleb.

The boy who once hid behind books and expectations.
The boy who chased a dream so far, he almost lost
himself.
The boy who found his way back—*to her.*

She could see it all in his eyes.

The fear. The hope. The *love.*

And suddenly, it wasn't so overwhelming anymore.

Suddenly, it was the easiest thing in the world.

A breath.

A heartbeat.

Then—

**"Yes."**

The hall *erupted.*

Applause, laughter, shouts of celebration—cheers from their bandmates, from Sophie and James, from people they hadn't even spoken to in years.

Somewhere, in the midst of it all, *their* song played softly in the background.

And as Caleb reached for her hand, lacing his fingers through hers, she realized—

This was never really an ending.

It was only the beginning.

The cheers rang in Caleb's ears, but he wasn't really hearing them. The applause, the laughter, the music—it all blurred into the background as he looked at her.

His *wife.*

His fingers tightened around hers, grounding himself in the moment. He exhaled, a small, disbelieving chuckle escaping his lips.

Then, barely above a whisper, just for her—

**"We did it."**

She looked up at him, eyes shimmering under the golden light, her lips parting in a soft laugh—one of relief, of happiness, of *finally*.

And just like that, nothing else mattered.

Not the past. Not the years they lost.

Because they had made it.

Together.

# Epilogue

Time had moved forward, as it always did. The late-night conversations, the fleeting glances, the quiet moments filled with unspoken emotions—all of it had become memories, tucked away in the corners of their hearts.

Life had taken them in different directions, pulling them apart, then unexpectedly bringing them back together. It wasn't immediate, nor was it easy. Years passed, paths crossed, and slowly, what once seemed like a chapter closed forever turned into something new.

Caleb stood at the altar, his heart pounding—not with nerves, but with the overwhelming realization of how far they had come. He had imagined this moment countless times, yet nothing could compare to seeing her walking toward him, eyes filled with the same quiet warmth that had once made him fall in love without even realizing it.

Lily had always been a mystery to him—soft-spoken yet deeply expressive, hesitant yet brave in ways he could never be. And now, standing there, about to say the words that would bind them together forever, he knew—he had always known—that it was meant to be.

James and Sophie sat in the front row, exchanging glances, as if silently acknowledging how unreal it all felt. They had drifted, lost touch, let life take them where it wanted, but somehow, in the end, the four of them had found their way back—different, older, but still connected by the moments that had once defined their youth.

As Lily reached him, she smiled—soft, beautiful, and filled with a thousand untold stories. And in that moment, Caleb knew that everything they had been through, every twist and turn, every moment of distance and silence, had led them here.

Because love, real love, doesn't fade. It waits. It grows. And sometimes, it finds its way back when you least expect it.

And maybe, just maybe, this was always meant to be.

Darsha S Nair, a gifted young author and creative spirit, has captivated readers with her debut novel, *Maybe This Is Love*. Beyond writing, she is an exceptional student with a deep appreciation for literature and storytelling. Her novel delicately explores young love, friendship, and personal growth, capturing the emotions and experiences that shape us. With a sincere passion for writing and a keen understanding of human connections, Darsha embarks on a promising literary journey, hoping to touch hearts and inspire readers along the way.

www.ingramcontent.com/pod-product-compliance
Lightning Source LLC
Chambersburg PA
CBHW051143130726
47988CB00005B/1962